FORBIDDEN

AN ALEX CONNER CHRONICLES
NOVELLA

OTHER BOOKS BY THE AUTHOR

Trust: The Alex Conner Chronicles Book One
Truth: The Alex Conner Chronicles Book Two

FORBIDDEN

AN ALEX CONNER CHRONICLES
NOVELLA

BY
PARKER SINCLAIR

RAWLINGS BOOKS, LLC

Rawlings Books, LLC
Visit our Web site at
www.Parker.Sinclair.net/RawlingsBooks

Printed in the United States of America

Cover Art by Mike Dine
Edited by Meredith Tennant
Book Design by Maureen Cutajar

Paperback Edition ISBN 978-0-9908565-7-3
EPub Edition ISBN 978-0-9908565-8-0
Mobi Edition ISBN 978-0-9908565-9-7

For my friends and family.

Dreams do come true when you take the leap
and push fears away.

Acknowledgements

To Rhonda Byrne and her books *The Secret* and *The Magic*. These books changed my life for the better and I am a much happier and productive me!

To my editor, Meredith Tennant, for keeping up with my journey and my own personal style of crazy.

To Mike Dine for cranking out another awesome cover.

To Kelly, Kim, and Amy for reading along with me and keeping me on track.

To Amy for being an amazing friend and a kick-ass sales woman.

To Club X—couldn't do this without you.

To Leslie—I know we will always support and push each other to greatness.

To Ang for his awesome social media know-how and creative mastery.

To Vicki Drane for being a creative publicist and supporter.

To Gon Carpel at ROAR and Morgan Page for allowing me to use amazing lyrics for my scene.

To Dave Stinson for his media mastery and for making me feel important and respected.

To all my fans for continuing to follow the Chronicles and for believing in me and loving the characters.

To my family for being the best cheerleading squad there can be.

Contents

A thrill, a moment
A time, a place
Begin your search
Define the way
Leaving was forced
But now I'm free
So find your path
Your path back to me.

– S.D. Shannon

CHAPTER 1

The Only Way

There's only one option I can think of and it's one I was forbidden to use. He told me never to contact him, to stay away from him, but how can I? Alex's life is at stake, so to hell with his rules.

Focusing on packing is a chore, which isn't the norm for me. A quick trip on a whim to Vegas, San Fran, or LA is a welcome escape that I delight in, but this isn't a play trip—not by far. The empty room where Alex disappeared is down the hall, and its memories from the last four days send foggy tendrils of despair toward me. I'm subdued, not my normal perky self, something that I don't wear well. I'm the peppy one and Alex is the serious, mysterious one. But the situation we're in is dragging us all down.

Alex's cat, Pitter, alternates between jumping on my bed, meowing in my face, and rubbing my ankles with urgent sounds. He knows something is amiss and, like the rest of us, he's worried about Alex.

It's been twenty-four hours since she literally slipped through my hands. I was sitting next to her when the room began to shake. The low lights trembled right before darkness crept in, and a howling wail terrorized both of us. I had my hands on her, I felt her skin on my fingertips, yet in the next instant an overwhelming coldness invaded my body and spread its iciness throughout the room. The abrupt quiet after the howl was jarring and my teeth chattered—the room felt like a tomb. When the lights returned and I got my bearings to look around, the bed was empty. Alex was gone.

I pick up my phone and stare at the unlabeled number, the one he doesn't even know I have, nor have I ever dared use. Should I just show up in Virginia and wink at the guards in the hope that they'll let me into Quantico, purely because of my charm or merely because I'm wearing one of my barely there dresses? Those tactics may work for me in San Diego, but my powers haven't been tested on FBI agents and Marines. I yank a few of my tight-fitting dresses off their hangers, knowing how my curves will look swaying toward the gates, and maybe, just maybe, the right rookie will raise those gates for me.

To be honest, my real power lies in being a Seer. Alex says that my vixen skills are just "icing on the cake." As a Seer, I go into visions that show me what has happened in the past, what is happening now, and what may happen in the future. The emphasis is on the "may," as even the smallest of divergences can alter what is to come. The strongest of us can see multiple predictions at once—Seers like the one I'm seeking in Virginia.

I miss Alex. She's my best friend. I miss busting her balls, partying, and working with her late into the night. She is my complete opposite, with her tall, slim build and curly brunette hair. I, on the other hand, have what she calls the "bombshell package." Alex only just came back from months in the desert and now she's gone again. Not only have we been working together for years in the party-planning industry, we've also become honest and open with each other about our powers, using them to take on evils in the world. The word "honest" sends shivers through me; I have not been completely honest with anyone, not even my best friend.

I can't help feeling like I failed Alex by not locking on to the danger that lingered inside Justin, her on-again-off-again boyfriend, or the "I warned her about him boy toy" as Dana has been quipping multiple times since Alex went missing. At Alex's request, I tried to use my skill to sense something in Justin, but I didn't pick up even the tiniest tendril of deceit. Looking back on it now, that absence should have been a warning. No one is that "good" and even the most well-meaning person can choose a path that leads them toward darkness. The only thing I can hope for now is that the skills she has proven to have will keep her safe.

"Sandra? Sandra, are you still here?" It's Dana, the Mistress of Potions and Weaponry herself. She's been having me retell over and over again what happened before Alex disappeared. Not to mention the smelly herbs and smoke that she's been passing over the bed Alex was in, in hopes of finding her or maybe reaching out to her. Ryan left to ask the Council for help and Valant turned up right after Alex disappeared, too late, which had him way more pissed off than I would have expected. He'd say she was a prize of sorts for him, his little chaos magnet for him to feed off of, but I sense something else. Respect? Friendship maybe? Things I've never heard of in relation to a Demon. No, my Demon tales are few and far between, the one with my brother being the hardest and most painful to recall.

"I'm in here, Dana, just finishing up." Dana breezes in with a glass full of ice and brown liquor in her hands. I'll have to restock the bar. Not only can Alex drink me under the table, little Miss Mistress of Potions and Weaponry has been pounding down the cocktails like a hummingbird in a nectar free-for-all.

The clinking of the cubes reminds me of the wind chime on the back deck of our family beach house in Virginia. Will I ever see Alex again to tell her the real story of my life—of my childhood? I was different back then, a different type of free, a tomboy skating along the streets with salty, windblown hair. A far cry from the heels, tight dresses, free drink-getting girl that I am now. The echoes of waves crashing enter my mind and I'm momentarily transported there before the sound of Dana's glass coming to rest on my dresser summons me back to reality. Ice sits alone in the crystal prison, left to melt away all on its own. The sight has me worrying about Alex, seeing her trapped like the ice in my mind, left to waste away, scared and alone.

Dana's aged hands may look delicate curved around the glass, but I've seen her in action over the last few days and she is the epitome of "looks can be deceiving." Not only does her long, flowing white hair and affinity for regal dresses remind me of a mystical *Lord of the Rings* character, but the effect she has on every single powerful person that has been here over the last few days is a marvel, to say the least. At one point during the panic, when Alex was unconscious, Dana wedged

4

herself between Ryan and Valant and I saw fear in their eyes. Now, Valant is a full on, unchecked Demon and Ryan is a badass Earthen Protector, and neither run shy on power or machismo, but damned if I didn't see mental tails between their legs. Dana's been holding us together, for the most part, her calm yet gruff demeanor keeping us in check and focused. Yet it wasn't Dana who gave me the push I needed to go to the big gun for help. Nope, it was the Demon. I shake my head even now, wondering why I'm following his lead on this one.

I haven't heard the name Avalon since my brother and I were young. We heard stories about an ancient world where the Fae lived and thrived. They were children's stories our parents and grandparents told us, but when we got older it became more obvious that at least parts were true. So perhaps Avalon is a real kingdom and only royalty live there, well, until now apparently. Unless Alex is royalty? I mean, she is the first of her kind in generations, so an object to be sought after in a Fae court, perhaps?

Maybe that is what this is all about. According to Valant, Alex shouted out the word 'Avalon' from her mind. She said she was being taken there by some "he" we're not certain of yet. The only people around before everything went to shit were Justin and Valant. Justin is dead—something Valant did with his own Demon hands and saw with his own Demon eyes. Nothing I've tried to see has shown a different outcome or possibility. The idea of Justin wanting to harm Alex, or trying to abduct her, seems ludicrous after having known him for so long. He loved Alex, that I know, but I saw the vision of what happened that night and he was obviously not himself; whoever he was, his intentions were malicious.

With Justin gone, who else would have taken her? Was Justin possessed by a Demon, like Alex's father was? I have repeatedly tried to think back to the conversation Alex and I had before she left for Montana. She was worried about her dreams; Justin had something to do with them, but for some reason I can't remember what more she might have said. It's as if that conversation was cut short, or a section of it deleted. A feeling remains, though, a feeling that I'm missing a key clue to who has her now.

After Valant shared what he knew he paced around, his straight, thick blond hair flying around the tops of his shoulders while his entire being shimmered with ferocity. A darkness swirled around him, occasionally accented with maroon lightning sparks; freaked me the hell out, and I've seen a lot of crazy shit. Just when I thought he was about to take off again, he froze, then turned neatly on his heel facing me dead on. Valant didn't say much and he only had to say it once.

"Time to suck it up, my little all-seeing Princess Barbie. We need your twin and we need the Nanda-yi." And with that, Valant was gone.

My twin brother Logan is a Seer as well, but he's gained other powers, powers that he acquired at a great cost. Alex didn't even know about him until that Demon Valant let it leak. She thought I was an only child from San Diego, but none of that is true.

"Any deep thoughts you care to share, Blondie?" Startled, I jump at the sound of Dana's voice. I've been doing that a lot lately. It's as if losing Alex has taken me off my game. I've lost my touchstone. My focus wavers and I follow ridiculous tendrils of confused thought. It's an uncommon restlessness for me, and part of the reason I so easily took Valant's suggestion to seek Logan's help. What he said clicked in my mind and my thoughts cleared. It was the first time I had a real plan—a sucky one, but at least I can move on it instead of pacing around my home.

"Sorry, Dana. I was just thinking about the whole Avalon thing. I know the tales we were told as children, but I have this nagging feeling that I've heard something about it more recently." I throw the shirt I have been folding over and over again across the bed in frustration. Pitter makes quick work of jumping on the bed and attacking the shit out of the shirt. I'm right there with you, buddy.

"Why don't we try to go back through the last few days in a Dreamwalk state again and see if anything comes up? Strong magic is at play in this house and I think you've been intentionally robbed of some of your memories."

I shake my head as I continue to pack. "I'm still fuzzy from our last attempt and I don't want to waste any more time. One thing I know, and something that I'll never forget, is that all the stories we heard growing up are real. Logan told me before we parted. All the magical lands, people, creatures—those places our parents told us about—they're all real. Avalon is one of those places, and Logan knows something about it. I'm sure of it."

Dana picks up her glass again and frowns at its liquor-lacking contents. "Well, I'll keep working with Terra and Vex. Vex says he's been to Avalon before, but he just doesn't have the same power and strength that he used to have. The fight with the Demon in Alex's father really took it out of him. Terra and I are trying to help him recover the old bag of bones's mojo, but it's proving to be very difficult, and the one person who could help us even further is the very person we're trying to save." Alex has been so worried about Vex. She knew he was in bad shape after he and the Healer's leader, who turned out to be her dad's mother, were attacked by her dad in a Demon-possessed state. Alex had hoped to use her healing ability to get Vex back to his foxy self. Knowing her, wherever she is, she's still worrying about him. That's Alex through and through; when she cares about someone, or something, she's fiercely selfless.

As someone with few friends, and no family except for a brother who wants nothing to do with me, I completely relate. Feeling the underlying urgency has me hustling to the bathroom to gather the essentials for a trip back to the east coast. It's been a long time since I've been home; my parents died when we were young and our aunt Aime, who cared for us afterwards, passed away years ago. So it's just Logan and me. Or rather there's Logan, and then there's me. We aren't much of a duo anymore, haven't been for a long time now.

"Do you think he'll help you? Your brother?" Hearing someone talk about Logan is not only rare, but also brings up feelings I don't often enjoy tapping into. My fingers absently grasp make-up brushes, lipsticks, and lotions; they barely register a sensation as they continue packing unguided. It's as if I'm numb to the bone, drifting back in time to when Logan and I were kids, when we were happy and the best of friends. These feelings don't linger long, though. It's hard to bypass the wreckage that blocks the road back to simpler times. I zip up my cosmetics bag and look up into the mirror. Rays of light from the bathroom chandelier hit my blue eyes and they shimmer. I can do this; Logan doesn't hate me, does he? I mean, after everything he's still Logan, still my brother. I tuck a short blond strand from my angled bob behind my ear and head back toward Dana.

"There's only one way to find out and a text message just won't cut it. I figure if I go all the way out there, he'll have to see me, right?" Dana shrugs, which looks odd on the Mistress capable of wielding some serious magic. She looks tired. We both are. All our attempts to use our Sight, Dreamwalks, potions, and wracking our brains to find another idea of how to bring Alex back have drained us. I'm not normally relaxed enough on a plane to sleep, especially since most of the time cocktails are served, and paid for, by new "friends," but I don't think I'll be able to stay awake on this cross-country flight. Not after all we've been through the last few days.

My eyes focus on the tableside clock; my flight leaves in two hours and it will take me a while to get down south to the San Diego airport. I pick Pitter up, soothing him and myself with a good-bye snuggle.

"I'm going to find a way to bring your momma back, big guy."

I set Pitter down, smoothing his fur, and grab my bags to follow Dana out of the door.

I'm not sure how this will turn out, but if I know Logan, and if he's as all-powerful as he was the last time I saw him, he may already know I'm coming. He hasn't stopped me yet. So maybe, just maybe, he will agree to help me—and Alex.

CHAPTER 2

Inseparable

I rarely fly into Richmond, although I did frequent the city quite often for the live music and the nightlife. If my family ever flew in and out of Virginia it was from the Norfolk airport, so it's a little disorienting when I get off the plane. However, many eager representatives come to my aid, at the lost look on my face, I'm sure, yet for some reason their eyes travel up and down my fitted jeans and tight V-neck t-shirt. Some women roll their eyes and huff, probably thinking I'm setting us back hundreds of years by allowing myself to be objectified. Ha! I just smile and shrug at them, and bounce away after the Southwest rep carrying my bags.

Richmond is two-and-a-half hours from where I grew up. We lived in Sandbridge, a small coastal community in the southernmost part of Virginia Beach, and considered the uppermost part of the Outer Banks. It's a community of nature lovers, surfers, fishermen, and, during the tourist season, full of people from all over the place. My parent's home was a three-level beach house, so Logan and I grew up with waves as the soundtrack to our lives and sand dunes as our backyard. The narrow streets and trails between homes were our gateways to a treasured community where we rode bikes and skateboards everywhere, surfed day after day, and spent a good deal of our time with friends who also lived along the beach and protected sound.

Our closest friends were Jax and Nora. Jax was a year older than Logan and I, and his sister Nora a year younger. Their whole family lived in Sandbridge, so we were close to their cousins as well. We all got in plenty of trouble together, from bruises to busted keggers, stealing lawn gnomes to partying in empty rentals and new builds. Despite scoldings from our parents, we were never kept apart long; the families always got together for cookouts, Thanksgivings, and birthday celebrations. In the spring and fall we went on camping trips down to the Outer Banks to fish, surf, and hold massive fish, shrimp, and crab boils with more food than our bellies could handle. Ya, we had a strong community growing up, but Jax and Nora's family were the only other Seers that we knew in the area. Nobody else knew about our abilities, and our shared existence made for a nearly unbreakable bond. My head whirls with memories, thinking how that all changed so quickly despite how many years actually passed. I'm only twenty-eight now, but I haven't seen Logan or Jax since we were twenty, when Logan left for Quantico's FBI academy and I headed to San Diego. Jax, as far as I know, stayed in Virginia to attend Virginia Commonwealth University's School of Medicine in Richmond. Nora? Well, no one really knows where Nora is. She and I were bubbly free spirits, inseparable tomboys that never let guys or drama with other girls come between us or stop us enjoying life. Besides, there was only ever one boy for me. After I lost him I couldn't bear to reach out and find Nora, and I have a feeling that if she wanted to find me, she would.

I didn't realize at the time that I would never look back to the east coast. Harsh memories cast a shadow over any glimmer of the joy, happiness, and wonder. Logan basically told me to stay away from him, and Jax would never look at Logan or me the same way again. Not after what he saw, and after what I asked him to do for Logan. Maybe I should have tried harder. I loved him after all, and I know he loved me. Jax, my Jax, and his amazingly touchable strong, lean body. Our days at the beach helped create his sand-blond hair, while his family shaped his southern charm and rugged persona that could haul in an eighty-pound tuna while also flashing me a smile that turned my girlie parts to jelly.

My memories have me nearly running into the eager airline assistant as he stops at the baggage claim carousel. Jax drifts away, back into that place in my mind where his memory can't cause me constant heartache and regret.

"Here we are. Is there anything else I can . . . help you with? If you're staying in Richmond I can tell you some great spots to check out. Actually, my friends and I are checking out a band tonight if you're looking for something to do." He's cute, his strong arm muscles bulging from his shirt, but all I can see in my mind is Jax. Plus, I'm not here for play. I take my bag from him and touch his shoulder lightly before lingering on his nametag.

"Thanks, Eric." Said with a subtle cock of my head and flick of the hair. "I really wish I could meet up with you guys. Especially since you're such a sweet guy and I'm sure tons of fun." My hand leaves his tag and the spell he is under lifts as his wide smile turns down slightly. I allow my lips to give a little pout and give him my best smile.

"It's all work for me this go round, but I'd love to keep in touch for when I come back." That works. He hands me a card and jots down his e-mail and cell. My bag comes into view and he snatches it for me effortlessly and walks me to the rental car area.

"Okay Miss . . . Oman," and on cue there's the wily grin I usually get from the boys when they say my last name like "oh man." It's pronounced "oh mon," but I let it slide from time to time. He continues, after a look that promises hot twenty-one-year-old boy toy sex drifts my way.

"You'll be in good hands with Tommy, and if you change your mind, I always have my phone on. Always." He gives me a wink and then walks away. Tommy is quick to upgrade me to a luxury SUV and I take a seat while he runs off to pull it up for me from the back rows. During the wait my mind returns to my childhood.

Despite our parents letting us run wild when we were young, they also worked tirelessly to remind us that we were Seers, and therefore exceptional. The fact that Logan and I were twins made us even more extraordinary, even formidable, so they worried that the bad forces in the world would seek us out. Aside from the evil Absolute Protectors, who want to be the only race in the world with the hope of bringing Gaia back to her true state, and not the one humankind has wrought upon her, our parents warned of other evils, temptations, and even the fear that others may have of us if they found out what we can do.

Due to their fears for us, they taught us to hide our powers more thoroughly than they had to when they were young. We weren't in the sort of Healers' community where they grew up, so we needed to be careful—concealed. Their fear hung on us, forcing us to lock away our powers for days, sometimes weeks at a time. Logan had the hardest time, struggling and complaining that he'd never reach his full potential. He wanted to join in the fight and help other people, but my parents convinced us it was only temporary and for the best. They promised we would go away for summers to live with other Healers where we could focus, practice, and—most of all—be safe. Jax and Nora were luckier, in more ways than one.

When we were fourteen we traveled alone to Washington State to spend time with Healers. We didn't know at the time that our parents were off on a mission to fight Absolute Protectors. Mom and Dad told us to keep our powers at bay until we got to the community. But by the time we got there, our parents were lost to us. Our mom and dad, both of them, were killed by a group of Absolute Protectors that overpowered them and their small group of Earthen Protectors in the Blue Ridge Mountains, not more than two hours from where I sit now. Logan never forgave himself, saying that if he could have foreseen their deaths, that could have saved them. I think part of him also never forgave them for forcing us to shut down. After their deaths, Logan never stopped using his Sight; he became more intense and focused, partially losing his grip on what was happening in the present as he lived in futures and pasts. The thing is, I think my parents knew the potential outcome, how can one not when going to war? Plus, as Seers, we are always taught that we cannot use our power to cheat death. Doing so can cause irreparable damage. In my eyes, our parents were heroes and they died fighting for what they believed in. They died for us. No, believing that didn't make it hurt any less or the grief to ever end, but it was a way to cope and survive—one that I think is much better than the path Logan took.

After their deaths, our aunt Aime came to live with us. Thankfully, we were able to remain in our home where she and our friends cared for us. Even though Jax and I had always been close, the tragedy brought us closer while Logan inched away.

Jax. My first crush, my first love, and my first heartbreak.

"What's on your mind, darling?" With a start I rise from my seat, looking around wildly, thinking I must have entered a vision. Jax's voice fills my head and warms me as I brush some of my darkest memories away, along with a stray tear that I didn't even realize had formed. My eyes focus on Jax standing no more than three feet away. He looks the same as he always did, but slightly more groomed in a button-up shirt and slacks. His top button is open and a tie loosely hangs in its place. He must have been at work. Damn, he makes a fine doctor. Jax is here, really here, standing right in front of me.

I take a step toward him as he closes the remaining distance between us. My arms go around his neck and my lips crush into his without hesitation. His tongue seeks mine eagerly while his hands possessively grip my waist. It's as if we never parted, that the damage was never done. The world drops away around us and I lose myself in our kiss.

CHAPTER 3

Love is Blindness

"Eh hem?"

Tommy has returned, yet I am lost within Jax's embrace, and my tongue is apparently lost as well. Jax breaks our kiss to address Tommy, who appears to be second-guessing the excellent upgrade he gave me.

"Hey, man. Sorry, but she won't be needing those keys after all." Jax rummages in his pocket and grabs some bills, passing one Tommy's way. I can't see what it is exactly, but Tommy seems pleased and walks away. I, on the other hand, continue to stare at Jax like a fool. His sea-glass blue eyes draw me in and take me back in time to when we were kids kissing on the dunes along the beach. He gives me his full attention again and the weight of his stare sends tingles along my arms, down my chest, and into places that long for his touch.

"Need a lift?" He releases me and grabs my bag and my hand as we walk toward short-term parking. I'm at a loss for words, dumbfounded that he is here, still wondering if it is true even though I feel his fingers entwined with mine, my lips still plump and tingly after our kiss.

Ever the gentleman, Jax opens the passenger door to his Tahoe and I slide inside while he stores my bag in the seat behind me before walking to the driver's side door. My neck swivels like an owl as I watch his every move intently. As a Seer, I shouldn't be surprised that he could find out where someone may be at any given time, yet why would he be focusing on me? And, if he does still care about me, well, as much as his lips seem to anyhow, then why hasn't he ever reached out to me? Then again, why haven't I reached out to him? I guess Googling, watching his medical career blossom, and calling his office number to hear his voice don't really count. Not to mention the weight of guilt bearing down on me that prevented me from ever trying; I mean, haven't I done enough to him already?

Jax starts the SUV without looking at me. I pout a little inside, seeing how far away he now seems. Get it together, Sandra, you don't pout about a guy. After getting my mind straight I shimmy into a straightened position, roll my shoulders, and pretend to straighten my skin-tight shirt a bit while skimming my breast. Out of the corner of my eye I see him glancing my way, that brief second curving my mouth upward as I put one hand behind my head, lean back, and exhale.

"You look good, Sandra. It's been a long time." Ya, too long.

"Thanks, Jax. You, too. Richmond seems to suit you, although I'm sure you must miss the beach." Great small talk. I wonder how long this will continue before I find out why he is really here and what is in store. My thoughts linger on crashing through the door of his house and ripping his clothes off, yet I am here for a purpose and Alex is more important than my passion for this man. For now, anyway.

Jax smirks as if he's reading my mind and signals to get onto the interstate as we head north on the 95.

"I know you're here to see Logan, Sandra. But why now? It's been years since you've been back. And just when things were falling into place. But I guess it makes sense. You and Logan always find a way to throw my life off track." And there it is. I knew we would get down to it sooner or later. I mean how could we not. I lost the love of my life because of Logan and what he did to save me. We promised Jax we would leave him alone forever. Yet here I am in Jax's car, going to see my brother who I have a "no contact" pact with. I'm oh for two so far.

"I'm sorry, Jax. I did as you asked; I've stayed away from you for years. And for the record I didn't call you for a ride; you just showed up. It's not as if you have to be a part of this." Jax stiffens at my words and I find myself staring at how gorgeous he looks even when he's pissed off. A tingle comes into my awareness as I backtrack the words I used. Oh shit.

"Actually, Sandra, I do have to be part of this. It's one of my Seer responsibilities. I keep track of Seers coming and going from the Mid-Atlantic area. And who pops up on my radar? Oh, my ex who is not only coming here, but who also plans on seeking out the one person I'd hoped never to see again." So I wasn't on his radar the whole time? Damn. I square my body towards him and lean a little closer.

"You didn't seem that disappointed to see me ten minutes ago." I drop my gaze before looking up at him through my lashes. This look works on most men I cross paths with, but none of them are Jax. "I've missed you." Damn, I want to touch him, but his rigid posture keeps me at bay.

"It's nice to see you too, Sand. I've thought about you every day since you left."

"I've thought about you too, Jax. I just didn't think you'd want to hear from me—ever. So I didn't try. Should I have?" He looks over at me, his eyes moving up and down my body, warming me, and inching me closer to him. He quickly turns his eyes back to the road and I am closed off again.

"Your timing sucks, Sandra. If we meant that much to you, you should have tried before now." He's right and I have a feeling that the kiss in the airport may have been on impulse and perhaps something he wasn't supposed to do.

"Are you with somebody? I mean, why wouldn't you be?" Jax made all the girls swoon. We went to Virginia Tech together, but I never worried about him. He was focused on his studies, the soccer team, and on me. How did I ever let him go? Before he could answer, tears begin to fill my eyes because I know in my heart what his answer will be.

"I'm too late. Right?" He doesn't look at me but I can see the strain on his face. "I should have fought for you, but I knew what we did was unforgiveable. I knew it meant that you would never look at me the same again and I couldn't bear it. It seems selfish now, but at the time I really thought I was doing what I should. I guess I was wrong." Tears are falling rapidly now and I swipe them away angrily. It's been a long time since I let a man make me cry. My stupid ex-husband,

20

rebound, that might have been me paying penance for what I did to Jax. Why else would I latch on to a piece of shit?

"Sand, we don't need to talk about this right now. Let me get you to Quantico. I'll stay nearby in case Logan refuses to see you . . ." A phone call interrupts him and we both look down. A gorgeous woman flashes across his screen. Her stunning features, long dark hair, and cocoa skin look back at me and I know. Jax has moved on and this woman now has the love I left behind.

Jax hits a button and the phone stops ringing throughout the car. Her picture remains though and my heart drops. It feels like the day I left. My heart torn apart again and it's my own damn fault. I steal one more glance his way and hope my eyes aren't deceiving me when I see a torn look on his face. Maybe their relationship is new or maybe, just maybe, he doesn't love her and he never stopped loving me. I don't pry; instead I look out the window as we drive north, thinking of the past and how we got to where we are. I have tried to compartmentalize it for so long now, but with Jax here and Logan not far away, I need to prepare.

I have to go further back than when we parted. The shitstorm began when Logan and I were twelve, and our parents were still alive. Our father's mother came to stay with us for a while. She had become ill and frail, nearing eighty-five years of age and weathered by time, a life well lived, and bearing and raising two children on her own. We loved her, trusted her, and would do anything for her. But this time she was different. Dad kept telling us she was not going to be around much longer and to try to make the most of our time together, that her age and medicines had made her act a little different but that she was still our Nana.

One night when my parents were out on a date night, Nana came to Logan and me and asked us to sit with her. We gathered around her chair in the living room where a fire crackled and a blanket covered her legs.

"I fear my time with you all is at an end. I'm losing the fight to stay." Logan and I each grabbed a frail, bony hand, and sniffled back tears.

"We love you, Nana, please don't leave us." My head was down when she reached for Logan's face. Her movement stirred me and I looked up to see his intense eyes, eyes like stone, grey stone mixed with mother of pearl. He refused to let any tears fall and instead appeared to be trying to find a way around her impending death.

"Perhaps you can save me, my dears. Find the Nanda-yi totem. It will heal me. I will be able to stay with you forever." Of course we wanted to save her; she cared for us and taught us, plus she was our father's mother. Logan's face changed, changed in the way it did when he refused to take an answer for what it was. It was his determined face that sometimes got us both in trouble, but usually meant that there was no holding him back.

"But Nana," I protested, "you and Mom and Dad have taught us that death is a part of life and that we should celebrate when our loved ones join Gaia. You're never really gone, right?"

Nana was definitely not herself. When she visited us last she was singing songs to us about the afterlife for a Seer, when she would be able to help create the power that her children, grandchildren, and great-grandchildren would use. She had wiped my tears, telling me that she would always be with us.

Now she was asking us to go against nature, to go against what we had been taught as Seers—she wanted us to cheat death.

While I was torn and confused, Logan was all business. "What is the Nanda-yi, Nana? I'm sure I can find it for you. Tell me how." I started to object but I caught Logan's glare and backed down. My Nana's hand remained on him; she didn't look at or touch me at all. I'd seen Logan like this, but solely in the name of research and curiosity. He had to know that we couldn't do this; I trusted that he did. Of all the people in our world, I trusted Logan the most. Whatever he was doing had to be for a reason. But I still checked my pocket for my phone in case I needed to call our parents.

"Let me show you instead," replied Nana. "I think you may already know just where to find it. It has to be taken, my dear children; you cannot borrow it, only possess it."

I gasped as we got sucked into her vision, my twelve-year-old mind spinning around wildly, not used to it happening so quickly. Nana's visions were usually so warm, slow, and comforting. This one was not.

When things began to clear and I took a look around, I knew exactly where we were: Jax's room. Nora and I had messed with him just the other day by flipping pictures upside down and turning his little soccer trophy guys around so their butts faced outward. I used Nora's mom's bright red lipstick and made one kissy mark on his mirror, not thinking at the time that kissing the full length mirror at my full height would match his face exactly, since we were head to head at that age. When Nora saw it she laughed hysterically, which not only made me flush crimson, but also gave us away. Jax came tearing into his room, chasing us out before I could wipe away the evidence. He never said anything about it, but when I came over the next time, my lips were still there.

I warmed at the memory despite the coldness of the vision. I expected to see Jax running in but instead, Nana pointed a bony finger at a statue high on his bookshelf. My stomach dropped when I realized I knew exactly what she was showing us. Jax's most prized possession, a gift from the man who had saved his life.

Jax's family is originally from Australia, and when he was six, his parents took him there for the first time. During a camping trip he wandered off and became lost for days. He was near starvation and death when an Aborigine named Yilee found him and brought him into their nation to heal and care for him, even though he was an outsider. Jax talked about him as if he was a second father, and Yilee called Jax his son.

Yilee gave Jax a carved wooden totem of their tribe's spirit animal, the wedge-tailed eagle. It was a strong and commanding-looking bird, with its wings spread. Jax called it his "spirit guide," telling us that the eagle was a gateway to "True Sight." Yilee told him that the totem symbolized open-mindedness. Its purpose was to remind the owner not to live in a closed-minded world, but rather to care for others.

Since Jax's savior passed away, the eagle was his only link to the man who had rescued him and adopted him into his nation. We couldn't take it from him, could we? Even for our own grandmother? Isn't death the natural course of things? Seers have always been taught that we cannot stop death and we should not fear it. To try to change the natural order would bring us closer to evil, to darkness, and my family was all about helping others and living life in the light. Jax never even called his carving Nanda-yi, at least not that I could remember. Yet when I turned to Nana, the thirst in her eyes was enough to let me know that this was the totem she sought. One that she hoped would help her heal and stay with us forever.

My grandmother's wish was confusing to Logan and me, but we loved her and she had never led us astray.

When the vision disappeared she whispered in Logan's ear before speaking to us both. "Dears, the Nanda-yi is very powerful and must be taken by an equally strong Seer. Your combined strength will be more than enough. Once you possess it, and you gift it to me, I can be healed. Won't that be wonderful, darlings? I'll have so much more time with the both of you."

Nana smiled at us and then excused herself to her room. I tried to convince Logan that taking this from Jax was a terrible idea, that he was our friend who would be devastated if it went missing. When that didn't work I appealed to him as a Seer and that death wasn't something we should seek to prevent. Logan, ever the seeker of knowledge, tried to tell me that things were changing, that we knew so much more and had so much more power. Being constrained by the old laws wasn't necessary. Plus, she was family. We had to help her.

Reluctantly, I agreed and Logan and I crept into Jax's house when we knew they were away for the weekend. We always watched each other's houses when anyone was away, so we entered their back door using the spare key we kept on our key hook. Birds rustled in the Back Bay woods, seeming to give warnings as the door shut behind us. Jax and Nora's house backed up to the sanctuary, which was pitch dark and covered with brambles of overgrown wildness and teaming with critters of all size, shapes, and leg count. We passed through their downstairs living room and down the hall to where Jax and Nora had their bedrooms. Most of the house was upstairs, the possibility of flooding requiring most homes to stand on stilts with kitchens on the upper levels, just like ours.

When we reached Jax's room I grasped Logan; he turned to me with a wild look in his eyes, but he didn't stop, instead opening the door and leading me inside. Jax's bookshelf was across his room and my eyes immediately focused on the formidable, yet beautiful bird. Logan released himself from my grip, stood on Jax's chair, and reached for the totem, quickly passing it down to me. As I held the object in my hand it was as if the eagle gave me a quick shake of his head and focused his eyes back up on the shelf. It had to be a trick of the mind, but anything was possible. I glanced up at Logan and straightened my back. This must stop now.

"Logan, we can't do this. Not to Jax. It isn't right." My voice was stern. It was the only way to get through to Logan when he was in bulldozer mode.

Logan looked at me and back to the totem. "Something doesn't feel right when you touch it, does it?" Logan's voice was panicked and shaky. I didn't feel anything when I held the Nanda-yi, but Logan seemed frightened of it. I moved around him, climbed on Jax's desk chair, and placed it where it belonged.

"Nothing ever felt right about this, Logan. I think we need to talk to Mom and Dad. Don't you think Nana is acting

26

strange?" Now that we weren't near her, clarity seemed to seep into Logan's awareness.

"Yes, the Nana we know wouldn't ask us to do this, and she kept telling me to not listen to you. Why would she do that? She made it seem like you were holding me back, but I know that isn't true. I knew it when she was saying it, but I kept latching on to wanting her to live. It was like the idea of her strangeness didn't linger and the need to save her overtook me." He looked down at his hands, staring at them like they were dirty. He even wiped them off on his jeans and then shook his head.

"I'm sorry, Sandra, I don't know why I didn't listen to you. Something *is* going on and we *do* need to talk to Mom and Dad." Our parents were at a training in Washington, D.C., and the thought of returning home to Nana sleeping in the house alone with us frightened me for the first time ever.

We turned to leave Jax's room, but I looked back one last time at his mirror and saw my kiss mark still there. I knew we had made the right choice and I never doubted my instinct again. However, after that I did worry about Logan and how easily he could be influenced to do something that could hurt someone else.

After skating back home with drops of rain falling around us in the warm, humid night, we let ourselves back into the house quietly and huddled together in Logan's room. Neither of us could control our overwhelming feelings about Nana. We cried, feeling that we were letting her die, before falling asleep together like we always used to when we were younger. I woke to her hovering over us in the darkness, her eyes blazing. She spoke in a voice that was not her own, demanding to know where the totem was, even though we hadn't told her we were trying to get it that night—that was the one thing Logan and I had agreed on before we left for Jax's.

Logan was up, as still as stone, while I was trembling. Suddenly, Nana grasped the sides of our heads, pushing our skulls together; we were thrust into her vision of a dark room with only pinpricks, like stars, shining down in the otherwise sightless room. She told us to think of anything we wanted and within seconds, columns full of sparkling tiaras, gem-laden necklaces, and soft mewing kittens sprung up around us. Logan broke from my hold on his hand and ran toward tables arrayed with crossbows, small dinosaur toys that moved as if alive, and candy as far as the eye could see.

"Do you see now what can be yours, my children? Get me the Nanda-yi and I will share all this with you." I dropped the gorgeous baubles from my hands and walked closer to Nana. She stood taller than I had seen her in years and her body vibrated with excitement. With a smile, I had just turned to walk back to my treasures when I saw a hint of movement underneath the skin of her arms. I didn't give myself away and instead skipped over to Logan and pretended to unwrap candies, copying his actions and giggling. Logan smiled at me with chocolate covering his lips, but immediately noticed the look on my face and the word I mouthed, and dropped his sweets slowly.

Our parents had warned us about Demon possession. They warned us about their tricks and promises to give someone whatever they wanted, but that always meant the Demon would ultimately earn its prize and the cost was always high, always dangerous. Nana was possessed. I knew it, and when I mouthed the word 'Demon' to Logan, he knew it too.

Our eyes were hidden from the Demon impersonating Nana, so only we could see our reflected fear taking hold. I worked hard to control myself, knowing that we had to escape and the only way that would be possible was to not give ourselves away. Our parents' training to conceal our power also taught us to chameleon our feelings, so when I grasped Logan's hand we both locked away the terror to concentrate on getting the hell out of there. Using the combined power of our Sight, we left the Demon's vision before the evil being knew what was happening.

The instant we felt our feet upon the floor, and our swirling eyes revealed Logan's room, we took flight. Our hearts pounded violently in our chests as the fear that we had so craftily hidden away rushed out of us like a tsunami tearing through buildings, mountains, and trees like they were mere pieces of paper. It always felt like this whenever we kept our Sight at bay for days on end. The intensity, once unleashed, could be momentarily paralyzing and I thanked the Goddess for not immobilizing us tonight. The word 'Demon' blared in my head and tore through my ears as we raced toward our parents' room. We barricaded the door with their dressers; the task was difficult with our small sweaty palms and quaking legs giving way under the wood and upon the carpeted floor. Once we thought we might have bought ourselves a little time, Logan grabbed his phone to call our dad. Our parents kept their calm and didn't question our story because they knew there would be no reason for us to make up such a thing. They told us to stay put, to not speak to the Demon, and that help was on the way.

The Demon masquerading as our Nana pounded on the door and for all I knew it would be able to get us, no matter where we were.

"Logan, should we get out of here? Won't it get to us no matter how many locks we have on the door?" I was shaking and my words came out in a rush that only my twin could understand.

"Mom and Dad said to stay put. Help is coming. It'll be here soon." I tried to steady my heart, but I couldn't help my urge to flee. I had seen the Demon's powers in the vision; however, it obviously couldn't get the Nanda-yi itself, so perhaps there were limits to what it could do. I wasn't sure whether my mind was trying to convince me so that I would calm down, or perhaps I was making some kind of sense.

A faint whisper was heard at the window and we spun around, fear of being attacked by a Demon heavy on the both of us. The banging persisted on our parents' door though, so we could only hope whoever was at the window was the help we were waiting for. A tall woman with bright blond hair pulled into a ponytail stepped through the window and put a finger to her lips. She pointed to the door and we both nodded, knowing she was asking if the Demon was on the other side. She had the air of other Earthen Protectors we had met during summers of training, and her eyes sparked a gemstone-blue blaze that shimmered and danced along her irises while her fingers reached toward the floor. Blue fire climbed and curled around her fingers and arms like a mist and she waved her right arm to the side, forcing both dressers away from the door.

"Stand back, you two," she hissed, and in the next instant the door flew open. Logan and I were frozen in place, more in awe than fear, I think. This woman was a sight to behold—a warrior. As one we stood together and the Protector called for Nana to be set free. Well, in more colorful words, of course.

"Demon! I'll give you one chance and one chance only to go back to wherever your evil ass came from, and let this woman go!" We watched in horror as Nana's body and face contorted horribly as the Demon came toward us. At first I thought it was being forced out of her just by the Protector's words, but instead a face not her own pushed its way to the surface of her skin and laughed at us. In less time than it took me to blink, our blond heroine released her flame at the Demon and we screamed, fearing it would hurt Nana.

Instead, the blaze seemed to allow Nana to regain control of herself and the Demon's hideous features disappeared. Nana joined the Earthen Protector's demand for the Demon to leave her body and soon a red, oozing cloud separated from her body and stood there in a form half man and half mangled beast. Its legs were bent at odd angles and its fingers were long and tipped with sharp claws. It took one final breath to speak, but I found my voice ringing out singular and true.

"Demon, you are not welcome here. Return to where you came from!" And with surprise in his eyes, his body swirled in on itself and disappeared. Everyone was looking at me then, but I didn't think much of it at the time. I thought we had done it together. But apparently I was the final nail in the coffin—I was the one who vanquished him and he would not easily forget.

The Earthen Protector helped Nana sit on the bed and then finally had time to introduce herself as Alana. It wouldn't be till many years later that I met nearly those same eyes in Alexis, not realizing the connection until we started to share the truth of each other's special gifts. Eyes that I have kept so much more from than this encounter with her mother.

Alana called in a Healer immediately and Nana was cared for and put to bed. Our parents were home less than four hours later and thanked Alana and the Healer for all they had done. Alana looked at me and then said something quickly to our parents. Surprise flickered across their faces, but they never turned my way. I did, however, catch my parents' last words to her.

"Please let us know if we can ever help you as you have helped us." And with that, Alana was gone. Time and distance have me looking back on this scene carefully, wondering if she had made the call to my parents that led to their death. It matters not, of course. Whether it was Alana or not, my past won't change and I don't need to revisit the sadness to know the truth—it wouldn't change a thing.

Logan and I didn't know till much later, till it was too late, that Jax's war eagle, the Nanda-yi, had other meanings and a hidden power. A power that was only tapped into when its holder's intentions were to appease the needs of an evil entity—no matter what was at stake.

CHAPTER 4

Possibility

"It wasn't supposed to be this way." My words are a whisper while my eyes focus on the Virginia scenery surrounding us. Green floods my vision. It is a different green from the San Diego desert. Palm trees have been replaced by pines that reach toward the sky. Other massive trees with broad leaves blur into one as Jax's SUV roars toward Quantico.

Even though I can't see Jax, I know he heard me. "No, this wasn't how things were supposed to go at all. Not the way I saw it, anyhow." I whip my head toward him in surprise. Had Jax used his ability to see into our future? Together? Doing things that we consider frivolous are forbidden for Seers, but maybe Jax hadn't cared. Part of me enjoys that possibility while another part fears it, after what happened to Logan.

"No, I didn't use my Sight, only my hope for our future." He smacks his steering wheel, something his pressed shirt didn't lead me to imagine him doing. Although, that tie all askew was sexy as hell. "Damn it! Why didn't Logan come to me for help?" He knows the answer. He had screamed it at Logan before he disappeared from my life. Regardless of what I know he remembers hearing from Logan, I think he needs to hear it from me again.

"I don't think he wanted you to get involved, to get hurt. I guess that happened anyway though, didn't it? What hurts the most is when people don't live up to your expectations." Looking at him makes my ears thump. Our years together keep flashing across my mind; his hand in mine, on my face, and the touch of the warm Virginia sand on my naked back as we made love.

When he speaks the good times vanish. His voice is laced with disgust and regret. "Is it too much to ask for my friends to ask me for help so maybe they don't become murderers?" His "s" stings like a slap in the face. My eyes look to his phone; I feel a tingle of happiness that he has someone in his life. Jax is making it clear that he will never forgive me, no matter how much promise that kiss had seemed to hold.

"No, it's not," I whisper, looking down at the pristine floor mat. Its flawless black threads tell me that he hasn't been to the beach much, that's for sure. He has changed, no longer the surf-and-skate, free-living boy I remember. It is stupid of me to think his kiss means something more. Too much time has passed. Seven years of silence, my failed, desperate, childish marriage, and now my devotion to my friends, my craft, and myself don't leave room for him, anyhow—right?

"I know he's your twin, Sandra. But did you *have* to help him? Don't you think he could have taken care of himself?" No, I don't. That was never a possibility. Jax didn't see what I saw. Jax wasn't there to see anything except what that Demon

34

wanted him to see. If the Demon couldn't have my life, he would ruin it, and that's just what he did.

"I don't know, Jax, Logan said there was no other way. I'm so sorry. I'm sorry about what happened, I'm sorry we disappointed you, and I'm sorry I lost you."

"Ya, me too, Sandra." Silence surrounds us again and the signs for Quantico start to become more frequent until Jax's signal begins to click and we take the exit toward Logan.

My body warms to the point of discomfort. Now that I am nearly in front of Logan I am totally freaking out about his reaction. He hadn't told me what would happen if I came back into his life, but he sure as hell made it clear that we were not to see each other again. I don't know if I remind him of the horror, if he blames me, or if he worries, just as I do, that what we did would somehow get out if we are together.

Stop it, Sandra. You did nothing wrong; neither did Logan for that matter. This was the Demon's doing.

Great, the talking to myself about what happened had stopped years ago, but now it's returned along with this intense heat and the need to scratch at my arms. Jax notices my distress and slows to pull over.

"Do you have to go to Logan? Is there something you need that I can help you with instead? Are you in trouble?" Damn, my heart aches with want. I wish to tell him everything and have him hold me and make this all better, but no matter how strong and adept Jax may be, he isn't battle hardened like Logan. He doesn't have my resources, or Logan's experience with Demons, or the stories of Avalon.

"It's not me, Jax, it's my friend. Trust me, I want you as far from this as possible. You should go home after dropping me off. Go home to her." I make a pointed look at his phone and turn from him.

"She's a good friend, Sandra, but I won't lie, I know she wants something more." I turn back to him, trying not to look eager, and focus more on my sultry nature to appear slightly aloof and confident. It is a Sandra he doesn't know and his face reflects his displeasure at my attempt to work the new me on him.

"You've changed, Sandra. Yeah, there are a lot of amazing changes." He eyes my body, lingering on my chest, and takes a deep inhale when he meets my eyes. "But I always loved you the way you were."

"You're the only one who knows that Sandra."

"Well, I've missed her." He moves toward me, and the heat from my imminent, and most-definitely unpleasant, encounter with Logan turns into delicious warmth that hits my cheeks and slides down my cleavage into my belly. My body clenches in my deepest places and I can't keep my face from showing Jax that I long for him.

He touches my cheek and then slides his hand down my neck. My breath catches as he peels my shirt partly off my left shoulder and leans in, kissing me from my clavicle down the rounded part of my shoulder and then back across the top of my chest. I freeze in place, trying to make sense of all that is happening. Alex is in danger, the love of my life is touching me for the first time in forever, and my brother has to be pacing like a tiger, awaiting my arrival. But for these few moments, I only want to care about Jax. His lips on my skin, the smells rising from his skin and hair, and how I can still recall the feel of his skin underneath my hands in the Sandbridge sunlight.

Jax raises his head and looks at me, his lips inviting me in and I will not say no. With his hand on the back of my head, I press my lips to his, softly at first. His mouth teases mine while his other hand lingers along my arm and across my chest. His fingers slide down the outside of my shirt and I moan into him as he allows his thumb to sweep across my nipple, causing a growl to escape his lips.

"Mmm, I like these," he manages between our lips meeting and tongues teasing at each other. My body reacts by turning toward him more and getting my right arm around his neck to move us even closer together. How I've missed these lips—to hell with his phone beauty, don't I deserve happiness? A chance at love again? A twinge of guilt sizzles through me when I think of him being happy after all he has been through with me, and how I would be the one to take that chance from him. What happens when he finds out what I am doing? The danger I am getting into, and the other life that has been taken? He won't want to be with me and I will have ruined his chances with the ebony goddess on his screen. My body wants Jax, but I also need to be open and honest with him before we both get sucked in. Jax catches on to my hesitation and pulls back, staring into my eyes and pushing a strand of hair behind my ear.

"I loved your hair long, but this is great, too. You were always comfortable in your own skin, but now, I mean damn, Sandra. You must have guys falling over themselves like toy soldiers." I smile back at him, not denying his words but also looking him in the eyes so that he knows he is the only man I ever really loved.

"Jax, I want to tell you everything. You need to know why I'm here, since I'm not sure you'll want to be involved once you do know. At least this time you'll know everything up front instead of being blindsided." Jax grimaces and shifts back into his seat.

"I've seen a lot as a doctor, and in my role as a Seer in Richmond. I think I can handle it. I'm not the same as I was either, Sandra."

"Perhaps, but you'll never forget seeing your best friend kill someone and your girlfriend help him cover it up, and that'll always be a huge wedge between us, won't it?"

"Maybe. Maybe not. Maybe it took me forever to realize that there may be more to it all. Maybe I'm finally ready to listen. Plus, it helps to know that you still have feelings for me; I think you might've missed me as much as I've missed you." This is my opening, my chance to explain all that happened that horrific night years ago. He wouldn't listen last time, too traumatized and misled by the Demon's mind games—mind games that just about destroyed us all. Before I can get another word in, a "whoop" of an alarm and flashing lights signals a military police car pulling up behind us. The marine, whose walk means all business and the promise of intense bodily harm should he be messed with, climbs out and walks to Jax's window.

"Ms. Oman? Dr. Ardell? Special Agent Oman is waiting for you just ahead. If you will follow me, please." We both nod stupidly and wait for the marine to take the lead. My mind turns back to Logan; Jax and I will have to wait as Quantico lies ahead.

CHAPTER 5

Quantico

I remember watching the Matthew Broderick movie, *Wargames*, like it was yesterday. The sadistic man-child computer takes over the NORAD base and nearly starts a nuclear war. I wonder if things will end as well with Logan and me as they did in the movie. Logan committed to the US government to work on their war-games technology, using his gifts to become an FBI analyst and fight terrorism. It is not only his sense of duty, but also penance for the guilt that clings to him for not being able to foresee our parents' death, and for what happened when we were barely twenty-one and the Demon returned for his revenge.

Our grandmother had recovered as best she could from the possession, but she passed away gently in the night six months later. It was a peaceful passing, one with dignity. Instead of letting it destroy us, we celebrated her life. We should have known from the beginning that she wouldn't try to cheat death. Our Seer beliefs were ingrained in our Nana's life as well as in ours, but Logan raged against them when our parents died. I wonder if we had gone to our parents right away and planned to destroy the Demon before it had a chance to bring the Nanda-yi and revenge into our lives, perhaps none of this mess would have happened. Hindsight is a kick in the ass to a Seer. Plus, something about Demon magic makes our Sight screwy anyhow.

We pull up to the gate and Jax puts the car in park as the guard approaches our Marine escort's vehicle. "I'll see you back at your hotel. Two Omans in one day is a bit much for me. Plus, I think you and I need to talk some more before I face Logan." Jax will have no part in seeing Logan right now, not that I can blame him one bit. The itching along my right arm makes it clear that I am not any more certain about this meeting.

Our escort heads back toward our vehicle and Jax rolls down the window to let the Marine know that he is ditching me here to face Logan alone.

"Sir, you and Ms. Oman can follow the road to the left and park in the visitor section. Special Agent Oman will be with you all shortly." The Marine looks over at me and I smile appreciatively. Not just at his uniform but truly out of respect.

"I'm dropping Ms. Oman off today if that's okay. She has my information should she need me to come back and get her. Would you like me to let her out here or still pull in?" Pull in, pull in. One last touch from his lips may be all my arm needs to silence its paranoid overreaction.

"Head on in and I'll let Special Agent Oman know she's waiting for him inside." Yay! The little subconscious me does a high cheerleader kick in my brain as the gate rises and Jax drives to a visitor's spot. Once in park, he grabs my phone and turns it toward me to enter my passcode. He quickly spins the phone back around and proceeds to add himself as a contact. Before I can react quickly enough to grab the phone back and enter it myself, his eyebrows lift in surprise and I know he sees his work number already in place in my contacts.

"Your voice was the closest I've been able to get to you for years." My voice is sultry and my body moves just a little, wanting to be closer to him again.

"To think I was happy whenever I didn't have long work voicemails, and the whole time I could have been even happier knowing you were still thinking of me." Jax inches towards me with his sea-glass eyes full of lust and promise.

"You forgot wanting you." He grips my hip suddenly and pulls me toward him, his lips hitting my neck and arching me backward. His other hand finds the back of my neck and tugs gently on the thick, short layers of my hair.

"I want to take you back home, not here, not Richmond, but back to Sandbridge. After you and Logan speak, can we go there before you take off again? I want to understand and I don't want you to leave again without giving me some answers." I freeze and red, pulsing trickles of danger flood my mind. I felt it with my ex and ignored it; why am I feeling it now with Jax? What's going on here? As if catching himself, he quickly adds, "Answers to where you've been and what you've been up to. Maybe I can help." His addition was rushed and I pull away from him slowly.

"What answers do you mean exactly, Jax? Why do I get the feeling there's more to you wanting to spend time with me then mending our broken relationship? What are you playing at and, more importantly, who are you playing for?" Jax gives me a look of a wounded man, but I know better.

"Was all of this a trick to get me to admit what happened that night? Are you trying to entrap Logan and me? Are you fucking crazy? Logan will tear you apart, and what about me? Don't you care about what you are doing to me?" Jax raises his hands, trying to soothe me with his soft eyes and smoky voice.

"I do have a job to do, but I'm not trying to snare either of you. You and Logan are two unchecked Seers and I was asked to bring them a report. Getting close to you now, here, is also for my own selfish needs. My need for you. I may have underestimated how much I'd feel when I saw you. I will bring them a report, but now that I've seen and touched you, I also want to try and mend us."

Grrr, secret puppet-master societies and records and accounts being checked and double-checked. I have no interest in the Seer Order and its attempts to have control over our lives. Jax told me he had a job to do here with Seers and I didn't ask for more details. That's my own damn fault for being caught off guard by his presence and that damn kiss. Now I can't shake the concern that he has other intentions. He was the one who told us to leave him alone and that he didn't want to see us again. If he had changed his mind, if he missed me so much, why didn't he ever reach out? I'm not the one who ended things. Nope, the boys were the ones who basically banished me from their lives. And now, when I step foot back in the state I may very well be wanted in, he magically appears and wants to forgive, all nice and easy? Best be cautious and stick with my plan. Find Logan, tell him about the Demon, find out what he knows about Avalon, and what, if anything, he can do to help us get Alex back.

I smile sweetly, play my fingers through my hair, and then pretend to adjust my shirt before responding. The temperature in the SUV turns up a notch and I know I have Jax enraptured for the moment.

"Let me see how things play out with Logan and I'll call you. I was hoping to go back to Sandbridge anyhow, but I'm just not sure when I'll be able to." I move my hand to his knee, touching him with promise and solidifying his confidence in my belief in everything he said. He quickly finishes entering his number and I take my phone, knowing I will have Logan check it out if he lets me spend more than a second with him today. I want to find out who Jax has been talking to and what he is up to. My heart tears a little at the possibility of his betrayal. There's been a lot of that going around lately, mostly targeted at Alex, but it also makes me more aware and reminds me to always use caution—even with Jax. I'm not the same twenty-two year old who ignored signs and felt like I was paying penance. No, I won't let a man fuck me over again, even if he has before.

I lean into Jax's space and speak so close that our lips touch. My breathy voice stirs the air between us while my words sooth him between giving him soft kisses with my plump lips. "Thank you for the ride, thank you for being more open to hearing me out, and thank you for this." And with the final tendrils of the "s" I give his lips an assault of "moms holding their hands over their kiddos' eyes" proportion.

I break free from him and allow my fingertips to linger on his cheek. What is he thinking? What will happen to us this time? My last thought creates a loud pop in my mind and I'm thrust into a vision so quickly that I can't tell for a moment that it isn't really happening.

I look around in the dark rain and recognize the storage facility from my haunted past. This is where Logan and I took a life. My head whips around to find exactly where we were on that cursed night, when I hear a faint gurgling sound. Dread constricts my throat; someone's struggle to breathe hits my eardrums over and over as well as the sensation of warm thickness on my hands. My heartbeat escalates as I look at my hands, covered in dark, hot blood. My eyes refocus further toward the ground where I see a body at my feet. Through the darkness I see the face of the dying man on the ground. It isn't just any man though; Jax's beautiful wide eyes stare back at me, gorgeous still despite his fear and sorrow. I manage to strangle the scream building in my chest and instead drop beside him and begin to frantically hover my hands over him. I don't know where to look or how to stop the bleeding. I need Alex. Jax flinches from my touch, his fear intensifying before his lips move to speak.

"Why, Sandra? Why?" I can't stop my head shaking from side to side and I can no longer hold back my scream of terror.

The vision kicks me out as forcefully as it sucked me in. My consciousness is tossed back into the car, my hand still on Jax's face and its silly post-kiss grin turning to a questioning smirk.

"Where'd you go? I feel like I lost you for a second." My eyes blink uncontrollably as I try to hold back the onslaught of tears my mind begs to release while trying to make sense of what I saw. I mean, really. What the hell was that? I have never been in a first person vision before. It isn't even supposed to be possible; it was like time travel and I am not Dr. Fucking Who. I stay cool though; no need to flip out. Of course now I wonder if the mistrust I feel for Jax is actually something else. Maybe I'm being warned about him to keep him safe, because after what I just saw—he shouldn't be anywhere near me.

"Just wishing we had a little more time to kill." *Nice choice of words, Sandra. Get your shit together.* My smile covers any proof of the crazy that has taken over and I give him one last kiss. "You'd better take off before you have another Oman to deal with. I'll call you." Just a minute ago I was ready to strip his background apart with the aid of the smartest minds in the FBI. Now, all I want to do is keep him alive.

With my suitcase rolling behind me and my bag on my shoulder I head toward the entrance. Before I reach the doors, a tingle shoots up my spine and I turn to see a hot shot with Brandon Lee looks running toward me, shoulder to shoulder with my brother.

They were obviously in the middle of training, dressed as they are in running shorts and short-sleeve shirts. Both have obviously hauled ass from wherever they were. Sweat is dripping down their faces, but neither set of eyes shows an ounce of stress or exhaustion. I look down Logan's right arm; the war eagle tattoo is in its place with sharp eyes, deadly beak, and wings spread wide, ready to take flight. He is definitely not happy to see me, calm though he appears, but I smile back at him and give an obnoxious "hey, bro!" to show that his pissy look doesn't bother me one bit.

Logan's compadre chokes on his laugh, drawing my attention back to him and his amazing arm muscles and black hair shining in the sun. I can't help but feel sad when I think back to the twin obelisks of father and son I paid homage to in the Pacific Northwest. Two stars whose lights faded way too soon.

"Man, Logan, when you say 'twin' you could be more specific about the fact that she thankfully looks nothing like you. Damn." I smile at him while reaching out my hand and introducing myself to the beautiful specimen that is making my reunion more tolerable in the humid Northern Virginia heat.

"I'm Sandra and I'm nothing like Logan. I'm actually fun to be . . . around."

"Now that I can tell. I'm Camden. If Logan doesn't show you a good time while you're visiting, tell him to give you my number. I'll save you." We both laugh at Logan's expense and it feels good to be around him and happy—even if he is waiting to rain on the feel-good parade.

Before I can say more, I hear Alex's voice in my head. "*Holy shit, Sandra, your brother is fucking hot! Like Brad Pitt meshed with Tom Hardy's rugged European ass hot!*" First, ew! That's my brother I'm, I mean, she's talking about. I sure as hell hope not some subconscious Freudian slip—gross. But I know that isn't the case. Nope, Alex is in my head! Shit! Maybe we have a connection after our intense magical visions together. I was also holding onto her when she was taken, so maybe, just maybe we were able to latch on to each other in some way. Of course, what a way to find out: our connection perks up when my brother enters the picture. Alex always has a way with timing, and with colorful descriptions when it comes to men.

Does this mean she's okay? At least okay enough to smart-ass her way into an inopportune time.

"*Well, it's your freaked-out vibes actually. Between your hot-and-heavy and then ice-cold encounter with Jax and now the Magic Mike scene outside of Quantico I have playing in my head, I was kind of called to you, and thank Goddess for that!*" Alex in my head is very difficult to manage with Logan looking into my very soul right now. His eyes are telling me to leave, but his jaw isn't clenched in anger, not like the last time I saw him, in the rain-soaked dark night. I, on the other hand, am smiling like a complete crackhead. Alex is alive; she seems to be safe or at least her same-ole self; now to find her and bring her home.

"Well, if you're here, Sandra, there must be something you need." I take a breath to talk, but Logan keeps speaking right over me. "Unfortunately, this isn't a good time. You're actually lucky I'm here at all. Most of my time is spent in the DC field office. I only come down to consult from time to time." Lucky my ass. Logan knew I was coming and made sure he was here for my arrival. Now he is putting me on ice, or perhaps just keeping me quiet until we have some privacy. I'm not an idiot, for fuck's sake. I'm not going to gush all over the place in front of Camden.

"*Give him a hug, girlie, get in there nice and close.*"

"*Shut it, Alex! Give me time to not look like an escaped lunatic after seeing him for the first time in six years, will ya?*"

"*Ten four. I'll just wait. Maybe. Maybe this won't last and I won't be able to help you find me. I'm locked up somewhere under some serious curse or magic. I haven't really been awake much, I can't remember a thing about why or how I got here, and when I am it's dark and I'm alone.*" Okay, I need to get Logan alone and now.

"*Hold tight, Alex. I'm on it.*" I let my smile fade and my features take on a serious edge to give Logan my this-shit-is-serious-shit look and I straighten up to show my confidence and determination to not leave here without talking to him about Alex.

"I'm sorry this isn't a good *time* for you, Logan, but you know I wouldn't be here if it weren't serious, so can I have a minute alone with you before you send me off . . . again?" That stung, I am sure of it. He nods to Camden and I watch him leave. Perhaps a little too closely judging by the annoyed sounds Logan is making to get my attention back. I suddenly feel parched looking at Logan. I've missed him; as inseparable as we were as twins, his absence from my life has been heartbreaking.

"I know about your friend, Sandra, and there's nothing I can do." Well, that shatters my reverie and instead pushes me close to his face.

"You aren't even going to try? Why? Because I came when you forbade me? I'm sorry that I've interrupted your little six-year pity party or fearfest or whatever it is, but I wouldn't have come if it wasn't urgent or if I didn't think you could help. Nobody else knows Demons like you do and I'm worried one has her. You also may be the only one fascinated by the idea of Avalon, and if anyone knows if it indeed exists or how to get there, it's you, so can we just let go of the past long enough for you to think about the possibility of helping me get Alex back?"

"Please keep your voice down." His hiss nearly knocks me backward, but I hold my position. Something in his eyes is telling and I think I may have surprised him with some info that his all-powerful Sight didn't pick up on when he was poking around. An intrigued Logan is a dedicated Logan. "You think she's in Avalon, and Alex is a she? I didn't see anything about your friend in my vision; it was like darkness covered someone when I tried to go back to when your friend was lost." I jump at the opening he seems to have given me.

"So let's go into a vision together and you can see her for yourself. I know she told me some things before she was taken that will help us find her, but I feel like something has been taken from me, too. Maybe you can help me get it back?" He taps his chin and I feel Alex stir within me. Do I tell him she can speak to me? My gut tells me to keep some things back for now. He needs to stay in the game or he won't play. No need to show him all of my cards at once.

"So, Demon or magical elven land, eh? Fine, Sandra, I'll bite, but not here. I can't have you turning heads and creating questions from my superiors here. I don't speak of you much—I can't risk it." I nod in understanding.

"Meet me at home. I'll be there early tomorrow." I wince and give him a confused look. His home in DC? The last home we had was sold when our aunt passed. It had angered me that he had gotten her to give him power over the house and sell it. I would have loved to keep it, but instead I was sent a massive check that I nearly dissolved with my tears.

"And where might that be? I haven't done much snooping so your sis is in the dark." His smile is impish and my heart blooms.

"Same place it's always been. Right on Sandfiddler Road." I can't control my right hand, which lands a punch on his muscular arm. I feel the pain and hear the pop as my knuckle cracks.

"Me likey! Strong and to-die-for looks. Not nice to keep him a secret, Sandra, along with many other things, I see."

Well, I guess I won't have to have the uncomfortable coming-clean talk with Alex after all; she can just glean it all from my own damn thoughts.

"You son of a bitch! Why didn't you just tell me you kept it?" Understanding and hurt comes quickly in answer to my own question. "To really keep me from coming back. Thanks for that, Logan. As if your scathing daily reminders before I left weren't enough, you had to let my heart break over losing our family home as well. Well, you wanted me to stay away from you and I guess to hate you as well. Congrats, it worked, obviously."

"You should at least be grateful." What a cocky son of a . . ."I would've told you eventually. I just need to be certain that we're safe. We'll talk more tomorrow. Third turtle, blow on the star on its blue shell."

"Huh? English, Logan. English." His damn smile stays in place during this entire exchange, probably more for the eyes watching than to reflect how he really feels about my pop in. He does manage a sigh though.

"The key, Sandra, it's where the key is." Oh, I knew that. I step back and grab the handle of my bag.

"I have a car for you if you need it. I have two here so you can take the X6 M." He points to a white BMW that looks fast as hell and right up Toretto's alley.

"It's not for your Fast and Furious enjoyment, Sandra. Just get there in one piece please." I take the keys from him and walk toward that steel siren that is aching to be ridden.

"Okay, so don't forget to bring him and this beauty back to SD with you, Sandra!"

"Calm down, I won't!"

"You won't?" Oops, talking to my friend in my head isn't the best move right now while he is entrusting me with his baby.

"I mean I won't harm your new toy and I'll get home safely." Logan looks at me closely and I turn from him, drop my luggage into the trunk, and catwalk to the driver's side. I see Camden a little ways away staring at me, so I give him a little wave before "accidentally" dropping Logan's keys and giving him a little show as I bend over. His groan in the distance lets me know that I was successful and hopefully he is only thinking about me naked in his lap and not so much about what is going on between Logan and I. Mad skills!

Logan leans into my window and I suspect he's praying that his car comes back to him. "I'll be good to her, I promise. See you tomorrow?"

"Tomorrow. Oh, and Sandra, don't tell Jax that you're headed down there, okay? Now isn't the time for a big reunion." I wonder if there will ever be a good time.

"I think he's ready to listen, Logan."

"Not now, Sandra." Logan's command is brusque and he steps back as I start the machine's engine. The roar rumbles through me and I can't help but be a little turned on by her power.

"Bye, Logan! Thanks for the car." It's the least he can do for being bullheaded, if you ask me. I give Camden one last wave before exiting the parking lot and at the stop sign my phone pings on the dash holder. I glance at it and see a text from an unknown number. When I swipe to check it, it has Camden's name and phone number along with *call me* typed below. Damn FBI and their lack-of-privacy-no-couth-having asses. It does make me smile though and I roar off toward the gate and back home for the first time in way too long.

CHAPTER 6

Coming Home

"*Okay. Spill it, Sandra.*"

I guess Alex is ready for me to tell her what I am up to, and what my past was really all about, but all I want to do is see if we can figure out exactly where she is and how to get her ass home.

"*We can worry about me later. Do you have any idea where you are or who took you?*"

"*No, not really. My thoughts get all jumbled when I try to think back, and I get really tired, like now. I feel so tired, Sandra; don't let me fall asleep. Keep talking to me.*"

"*I'm here, girlie. Can you hear anything around you?*" What I hear is a yawn echoing in my mind and now there is the light fuzziness that tells me her connection to me is starting to fade.

"*Alex! Alexis, stay with me. I'm getting help. We're coming for you.*" My thoughts reach out to her, but I can tell they are in vain. The connection is lost and I have to wait until she regains consciousness.

"Damn it!" I copy Jax's movements and smack at the steering wheel. I hate feeling helpless. I hate that Alex is all alone and that I can't save her right now. What I *can* do is stay focused on getting Logan to help, and that requires convincing him to let the past go.

The BMW purrs beneath me as I cruise down the 95. I'll arch my way east soon, passing the outskirts of Richmond, following the 64 through the tree-lined section surrounding Williamsburg, and across the bridges and tunnels toward the shores of Sandbridge. The music plays as the machine's smooth ride and soft leather caress me into memories I haven't relived in a long time. With hours ahead of me, I have plenty of time to weed through the past and mentally prepare for what awaits me when Logan arrives.

This won't be easy; Logan isn't the only one not looking forward to dealing with the past. Unfortunately, there is no way to move forward without diving in. The Nanda-yi came into our lives when we weren't yet teenagers; how could we know that it would return and dig its claws in—permanently.

When our parents died, Logan began to use his Sight obsessively. I worried about him, as did Jax and Nora, so Logan claimed to heed our advice and pay attention to our concerns. In reality, he just became an excellent liar and master at hiding the strain he was under. I think what really happened was that Logan found a way to keep his Sight on at all times, as a low-level radar. It came to him in nightmares, dreams, and visions. When the nightmares began about my death, Logan didn't share them with either of us. I should have known something was up when he transferred schools to join Jax and me at Virginia Tech. Jax stayed a fifth year due to red-shirting for soccer his freshmen year, and the extra classes helped him double major in biology and chemistry, which lined him up nicely to beat the shit out of the MCAT. Logan had been doing so well at Cornell, top of his class, but he claimed to miss being closer to home, and at the time I was just happy to have him with us again.

Once Logan arrived on campus, the three of us were pretty much inseparable. It was great at first, but then Jax and I realized we rarely had our own time. With our studies, there was little free time and Logan was always a part of it. When I tried to speak to Logan about it, he snapped. I thought he was just having a bad day because normally he seemed so at ease, but it turned out his ease had been all show. I'm sure his acting abilities come in handy with the FBI now, but to me, then, it felt like he hadn't trusted me enough to tell me what was really going on. Before he explained, he made me promise not to tell Jax anything, and then he told me about the visions he was having that were making him so crazy. Visions of me being taken and, in some cases, dying. He was only able to save me when we were alone, so Jax had to be kept in the dark for all of our sakes.

I still recall his face when I countered his logic. That was when I first realized how deep into it he really was, and how blind I had been to his on-going struggle with his Sight.

"Jax can help us, Logan. We can't keep something like this from him."

"Do you want him in danger too, Sandra? Is that what you want? I'm trying to keep everyone safe, so just listen to me and do what I say, okay?" His eyes were wild and I wondered how I had missed how tired he looked. The semester was ending and we were all graduating, meaning everyone looked spent, but he was worn, and I should have seen it. I tried a different tactic, one that rode on my hope that he was wrong. However, Logan was never wrong and deep inside the pit of my being, I knew it.

Despite his history of being a fucking know-it-all, I tried to insist that he let go of the constant alerts he set for his overworked Sight. Perhaps his devotion to making sure we were safe was instead driving him mad, or actually manufacturing the dreams out of sheer worry. Of course, Logan pushed all that aside. He claimed to have stopped terrible things from happening before and that we just didn't know what he had done. I feared for us: Logan, Jax, and myself. I mean, when your twin, who you know is the more powerful of the two of you, tells you he sees you die if he doesn't get there in time, I'd like to know who wouldn't be freaked out?

Logan assured me that he had it under control as long as he could get the Nanda-yi from Jax's room and wield it safely. I groaned. I didn't want that totem coming back into our lives; I even tried to use its need as case-in-point why this was all another hoax.

"It's the Demon all over again!" I pleaded. "A trick to get what he couldn't get last time. He must know how you've been using your powers, and he's turning your own obsession and worry against you. Can't you see it, Logan? It's the same thing he did before, only I'm the ruse this time, not Nana." This infuriated Logan; my words were a slap in the face. My words that accused him of being obsessed and misusing his abilities crossed a line in his mind. He was addicted to the power and control he felt, and I realized at that moment that I hadn't helped him enough. I should have made sure he wasn't still using his Sight in that way; instead, I blindly trusted him, maybe choosing to believe what I wanted to believe.

These memories bring tears to my eyes. It all changed so fast for the three of us, in mere weeks. I was in love with life, with Jax, with my visions for the future; I didn't want to die, and I certainly didn't want Logan to die trying to save me. Logan assured me that he would be safe as long as he had the Nanda-yi, and as long as Jax wasn't made aware of what was happening, he would be safe as well. The Seer code to not cheat death, and to not use the Sight for selfish reasons or gain faded into the background. There was no way I was meant to die for no reason. It wasn't part of my duty as a Seer, and as far as Logan could tell, we had only days before I was in danger. All Logan had to go on was a man's face and a feeling of dangerous power radiating from his being. He refused to agree that a Demon was to blame, stating that he would have sensed it immediately. He focused my attention instead on helping him get the totem. The Nanda-yi was the key to finding me, should I be taken, so he had to get it right then. The totem's promise of "True Sight" had never really left Logan, something I hadn't realized. When we spoke in his room he showed me countless pictures of the totem, and told me stories dating back to prehistoric times when the totem appeared in different drawings and was known by other names. He had printed other, similar, stories years ago, and his notebook containing every detail looked tattered and worn. Once again, he wanted us to take something from Jax that Jax cherished, without his blessing or help, and once again it felt all wrong.

Logan tried to play off his obsession with the Nanda-yi when he caught the look in my eyes mimicking Scully's concerns for Mulder's need to know the truth. Logan back-pedaled, focusing instead on his "real goal" and that *needing* the Nanda-yi so badly was to make sure I wasn't taken in the first place. No matter how many times he replayed the vision and tried to find the exact time and place, he could never stop me from being taken, only from being killed. He hoped that actually possessing the Nanda-yi and using its power would change things for the better. I only knew the totem as an object of a Demon's desire and to me that brought mistrust and fear. Logan assured me that as long as the holder and the holder's intentions were honorable, all would be well. I allowed myself to believe in him, but that didn't stop the constant worry. One basket case Sandra coming up!

I was a nervous wreck, and keeping everything from Jax wasn't helping. Jax knew everything there was to know about me, including every curve and freckle on my body. Here I was, hiding my possible death from him, each day. It felt wrong. I wonder if telling Jax would have made a difference, if we could have stopped Logan and thwarted this nightmare before any of it happened.

But it did happen, on a Thursday; my finals were over, Jax and Logan were both in grueling exams, and I was trying not to celebrate too early, or alone. I stared at the clock instead, wondering which one would be done first. When the knock came at the door, followed by Jax's voice, I jumped up at the thought of getting our celebrating on. I should have known before I even opened the door that something was off. Jax had a key so why would he knock? But, instead, I wrapped my arms around him and that was all I remembered until the rain woke me to my shivering nightmare in the darkness.

When I woke, I was sitting on soaked crates that smelled like rotting wood and cardboard. Aching arms were tied behind me, but thankfully my legs were free. My first attempt at moving caused my head to bang slightly against an uneven metal door that rattled on impact. I winced at the sound as my eyes and ears struggled to maintain some normality. Damn it. Had I been drugged? Not by Jax, there was no way that was him . . . why was I so stupid? Not a single lamppost worked, only a flickering battered light above me brought some clarity of where I was and what or who might be around. I was in a storage area of some sort. There were a few of them near the college for students to store belongings during the summer, and I could see an endless line of identical units leading in each direction from the one I was leaning against. Directly in front of me was an opening leading into the pitch black, mountainy wild. The sporadic light made my mind struggle even more for my wits to return. I needed to snap out of it if I was going to defend myself and help Logan when he arrived. There wasn't a doubt in my mind that he would come; this was what he saw happening, and with his power he wouldn't be wrong and I would be saved.

My pulse started to quicken and my ears strained to hear sounds besides the rain tinkling against the corrugated doors, creating mini-waterfalls all around. I didn't have to wait long. Logan's voice rang out in the darkness and I could see his frame walking toward me from the right. His voice sounded strangled, in pain almost, and I worried that this was another trick, and not him at all. Who or what can pose as someone else, or easily possess him or her? A Demon. I knew it! That was what that was all about once again and Logan was too blind to see it, and we both could die!

Oh god, I hoped the Demon hadn't fully possessed Jax, instead simply borrowing an image it knew would easily manipulate me into being abducted. I silently prayed for the latter to be the truth, knowing that allowing that worry to consume me would keep me from getting out of this situation alive.

I tried to stand, but whatever I was knocked out, or cursed, with must have been some sort of muscle relaxer. My legs were jellified and my back felt like it had been kicked in several places. Fear nearly crippled me, but I drew upon the last time I faced a Demon, and, if this was the same one, I clung to the hope that I was a bigger part of his banishment than I originally thought. I had to grasp on to some hope, so there it was.

A shuffling sound to my left alerted me and I squinted in that direction, flicking falling drops of water away from the dripping strands around my face. A form was moving toward me and I felt my heart pounding harder.

Logan, or perhaps his imposter, came closer and into the intermittent light. Relief washed over his face while his right arm jerked spasmodically. I tried to get up a few more times, readying myself to book it out of there no matter how wobbly my legs still felt.

"Back off, Demon! I can banish you with little more effort than wiggling my pinky, now that I'm coherent, you coward!"

Okay, so maybe I could barely wiggle my pinky due to being nearly numb in both arms after being tied up for who knows how long. It was light out when I was taken, so the beast had taken at least four hours of my life.

"Sandra, it's me. I told you I'd find you and keep you safe."

"Really, Demon? Your jerking-ass crazy arm is giving you away. Nice try though . . ." Logan's strong, powerful frame was closing in now and I got a better look at his arm, which was screaming, yes, screaming, and trying to fly away. The war eagle, the Nanda-yi, was no longer in its totem form, no, it had become one with Logan and the massive raptor was not happy about it. I squinted in the flashing light, hoping I wouldn't start having seizures like the kids watching Pokemon back in the day.

"You cursed Seer!" The unknown voice seeping from a hidden source in the wet darkness made my skin crawl. This was my captor. I could feel it in my bones and in my mind's reaction to his voice. "How dare you take the Nanda-yi for yourself when you were to bring it to ME!"

What the hell? Did Logan not tell me everything? I thought he needed to use the Nanda-yi, not get it for someone. Why did he keep things from me when I could help him, damn it! Logan sprinted toward me, but I was instantly lifted into the air and tossed further from his pumping legs and toward the source of the sinister voice. I skipped on my ass like a stone, feeling my jeans tear and my elbow skin shred along the asphalt. Despite the punishing blow to my body, I tried to get to my feet and run to Logan, but a hand grabbed the back of my neck and hauled me up to a standing position.

Each time I tried to get a look at the man holding me he shook me and took a crack at my kidneys. The fingers against my neck writhed and flexed, which nearly made me gag. This was a Demon all right and I had a feeling he had possessed another poor soul rather than just altering his appearance. Please don't let it be Jax, *please!*

Logan looked confused, but only for a heartbeat and then realization rolled over him and he smoothly moved into a graceful stride of confidence and immense power. As soon as he did, the bird quieted and I swear I saw its sharp, beaked face turn toward Logan before giving one last shake of its majestic body and retreating into his skin. I never found out back then what transpired and why the animal suddenly decided to work with Logan instead of continuing to fight its ass off. I am hoping tomorrow will bring some answers.

The growl that escaped the Demon's lips was terrifying, but despite my fear I tossed my head back hard, knocking his breath out by cracking my skull into his borrowed windpipe. I didn't have time to think about the person the Demon inhabited. It was life or death for my brother and me that night. As soon as my head hit, I ran toward Logan with all my might, falling into his arms for a brief second before he slid a knife through my bondage and pushed me behind him, using his own body as a shield. The power radiating off him was magnificent. His shirt was all shredded down the front as well as the arm, and my imagination reeled at the fight he and the Australian eagle must have had. Whatever the case, the bird was working with him now and I was certain this Demon's ass was finally going to be kicked for good. When I looked at the Demon I let out the breath I didn't know I had been holding.

It wasn't Jax. The man in the Demon's grip was a stranger, an innocent still, but not my love, and I was so relieved. I paid dearly for my selfish thoughts that night.

The man was possessed, that was for sure. The Demon pressed against his flesh, stretching and pulling behind the skin. The possession didn't appear strong. I remember thinking that the man would survive, just as our Nana had; all I had to do was send this Demon packing like last time.

"Give me the totem, Seer, or I will make sure you lose both your sister and your life tonight." The Demon cracked his neck from side to side and I looked more closely at the normal-looking guy he was possessing. I felt twinges of guilt cast a shadow over my confidence about what might happen to him if we didn't get that Demon out now. A dark haze began to ooze out of his skin, but before I could say a word to Logan the Demon created a ball of nasty-looking black energy between his hands and tossed it at us. Logan turned, and wings as wide as his body sprang from his arm and protected us. A dusting of spent power fell around us, but the Demon wasted no time before attacking us again. This time Logan and I ran, diving behind a pile of crates and springing out the other side.

"We can't hurt the man, Logan, he's an innocent. What should we do?" Logan looked to the bird on his arm, appearing to ask it something.

"It's the same Demon, Sandra, the one who had Nana." I was pretty certain of that myself, doubting it would be a different Demon making us pawns once again to get its hands on the Nanda-yi. This was no time for "I told you so" and I took my own advice and focused on fixing the situation instead of turning on Logan. In our world, it was probable that this would have happened no matter what, and at least in this scenario, we had some prior knowledge and control. It would have been nice if we could have prepared for a Demon; well, maybe one of us had.

Lightning crackled and shattered light against the mountains, giving an eerie glow to the landscape surrounding the barely lit stage of our Demon brawl. He growled again just before his hands smacked together, creating a gigantic ball of energy. I ducked, expecting him to throw it at us, but instead he lowered it to the ground, appearing to talk encouragingly to it as the blackness oozed in all directions. Logan hissed through his teeth and I feared for our escape. We climbed on top of the crates, exposing ourselves to another air attack, but we had to get off the ground and fast.

"Death covers all your escape routes out of here, Seer. Give me the Nanda-yi and I will clear the way for you." Logan reached behind him and I caught a glimpse of his hidden bag, worthy of the sly Peter Quill. He stopped with his hand behind him, eyeing the Demon with a wicked stare.

"Okay, Demon, clear the way and let Sandra leave and then I'll give you what you came for, again."

"Put the Nanda-yi back in its home, boy. Once I see my bird removed from your filthy Seer body, I'll let her go. No tricks now or I'll make kindling of those sticks of wood and have your flesh melting in an instant." I followed the creeping blackness below us, noticing steam rising from it like lava. Logan removed an object from his bag, a near-exact replica of Jax's war eagle in a basic, pure wooden form, without all of its paint and carvings. The bird had abandoned his wooden prison, choosing to join Logan instead. Something in me didn't want Logan to give it to the Demon. I felt the immense increase in power within Logan and I didn't think any good could come from the Demon taking it from him. I whispered into his ear, speaking softly, yet quick and determined.

"Logan, don't give it to him. I'm not completely certain, but I think we can get rid of him like we did last time." Logan's eyes darted toward me even though his body didn't move an inch. If it hadn't been raining, I would swear he was sweating profusely. Regardless, I could sense the strain in him of fear, worry, and stress from the eagle's attachment. I looked back at him with concern, feeling that we needed to get the bird back in its rightful home, regardless, or else Logan might be beaten down by its might.

Reaching out to him, I laid my hand on his other arm and squeezed it reassuringly. "It'll be okay, Logan. We'll contact the Healers and get help for you. Let's concentrate on banishing this devil for now."

"It's not going to work, at least not without a sacrifice. From my visions, I'd thought this was an Absolute Protector or, worst case, a Demon's illusion, but now he's possessed a man—someone who has nothing to do with this feud between us." I was confused at first, but then cold dread slithered down my back.

"Now, Seer twins," continued the Demon, "you have one more minute to decide or I will ruin you both!" He was bluffing and I knew it; he couldn't set us on fire for fear of losing the Nanda-yi, but something about Logan made me feel that this was never meant to end well. A smell of blood filled my nose as if I could sense the disaster already.

"Logan, what did you see? You have to tell me." This time he turned his head to look at me and I knew the drops rolling down his face weren't from the pouring rain, but tears of regret and sorrow. He touched my shoulder and turned back toward the Demon. He brought the wooden totem close to the war bird's image on his arm, and for a breath I thought he was going to give it to the Demon, but then as the bird began to stretch from his skin again, it let out a mighty cry and threw its head in all directions, screeching power out of its mouth and onto the ground. Within seconds, the lava had cooled and the boiling ceased.

What happened next was so fast I barely had time to think. I heard a car in the distance at the same time as Logan broke away from me, running full force toward the Demon. They both screamed, hurling their bodies against each other, with cruel, vicious sounds escaping them with a force so strong it was as if they were landing solid punches. I ran after Logan. If I could just get close enough I knew I could banish this Demon. Confidence surged in me as I saw the words falling from Alana's lips clearly, even though I had never heard them before.

"Sandra banished that Demon on her own."

If I was mistaken, the price would be too high to bear, but I had to try or we might all die. The man trapped by the Demon, my beloved brother, and I. I wonder if things would have been different if I had just stayed put. Did I need to be as close as I got? Would that have mattered?

The Demon soared over Logan and landed right in front of me. The man's eyes bulged as the Demon seethed beneath his skin, fighting to maintain his form instead of leaving the host's body. Why wouldn't he just face us as himself? As soon as the question formed, I was too late to find the answer. I started to scream out the Demon's banishment; it worked before, so I knew it would work again. Alana wasn't with me, but something in me knew I was strong enough. As I released the first word from my mouth, the Demon unsheathed a monstrous knife and pulled back, preparing to slice it savagely across my throat. My words came out in a rush, while I raised my arm to block the attack. I believed in myself; in my mind I saw the Demon being banished, so I closed my eyes and completed the command.

No pain came, only the sounds: a deafening thud of something hitting the ground, followed by a shrill laugh in the distance. I opened my eyes and Logan was hunched over the man's body. The piercing noise in the distance got my attention again and I saw the hideous Demon form laughing hysterically.

"You lose, boy, you lose no matter what! So powerful, but so easily manipulated. What will you do now? You are a killer. A *killer!*"

I couldn't look down again, knowing what I would see. Instead I stood straight and marched toward the Demon, flinging my defiant words at him again. "Demon, you are not welcome here. Return to where you came from!" He hissed and swore, but to no avail; he disappeared, leaving us alone with the destruction he had caused in the mountain rain.

What Logan screamed at me in the downpour was that the Nanda-yi was the key and it had to be taken in order to save me. This he was saying while the snarling bird writhed along his arm, blood dripping from where the eagle melded with his flesh, down along the bird's legs to the sharp, stained red claws that were deep in the heart of the dead man at our feet. At the time, I didn't know why Logan was ranting about the Nanda-yi when we were overcome with grief about the dead man, but now, thinking back, the eagle must have given him the power to overcome the strength of the Demon who was trying to slice my throat open, and kill him instead. The war eagle looked crazed from the fight, but when it caught my eyes it calmed before sliding back into its tattoo-like form along Logan's poor, bleeding arm.

The Nanda-yi clearly had some sort of control over Logan and I have always wondered if he would have been able to kill the man without it. The biggest question that haunted me was whether the man would have died at all if the Demon had still possessed him. Maybe not, maybe the bird could have damaged just the Demon, but I removed the Demon from the man's body, so I was to blame.

"We need to get rid of the body." Logan turned to look at me, the sorrow in his features nearly making me cry, but there was no time for tears. His headshake confirmed my statement and we separated. Logan went to get his car while I looked around the area for bags or old blankets to conceal the body. Logan backed up and we wrapped the body up before bending down to haul him into the trunk. It was all business as I tried to remain emotionless and numb to keep from going crazy. It didn't last long; my mind raged and became a fretting disaster even while my body kept moving to save our asses. I wondered if he had a family, if his parents or his friends would be looking for him. What would we do? How were we going to live with ourselves now?

"Sandra. Logan. What are you doing out here? I've been looking for you guys everywhere. Sandra's apartment door was left wide . . . *what the hell?*" Jax, oh god, Jax. What was he doing there? Damn it. He must have used his Sight to find us. I guessed he hadn't seen the entire gory battle or he wouldn't have been so shocked.

I went to him, but when I tried to touch him he pulled away. "What have you done, Sandra? You and Logan. Did you kill him? Why?" Logan tried to talk to Jax as well, but Jax's eyes shot down to Logan's arm, which he grabbed, yanking Logan away from me and into the flashing light.

"Why do you have my Nanda-yi attached to your arm?" Logan moved out of Jax's grasp. His eyes were wild with energy and I doubted he would give the totem to anyone, even his best friend and its rightful owner.

"Jax, let me explain, but later. Please, we have to get out of here and this isn't what it looks like." Logan used a quiet tone to calm Jax, but it wasn't working.

"I know what it looks like, Logan. It looks like my best friend and my girlfriend have been hiding some serious shit from me, so excuse me if I doubt I can believe a word you say right now. *That is a dead man!* Instead of calling for help you're covering it up, and that's something guilty people do." I moved toward him again, softening my eyes, putting all my love and pleading into them in hopes of soothing him enough to listen. When I got closer I saw a darkness creeping up his arm, along his neck, and into his eyes. It was the Demon's power; he was being influenced and I feared we wouldn't be able to break it easily. I got Logan's attention, using my eyes to show him what I had seen. He quickly realized the same thing

69

and worry coursed through both of us—we needed help and fast. I spoke to Jax, putting all my love into my tone and my words.

"Jax, this isn't what it looks like. We're calling for help right now from an Earthen Protector we know. She can help us." I touched his arm when I spoke, trying to seep visions of happiness and trust into him, but the Demon magic was strong despite his banishment. Curses and bad magic can linger like that, in the same way the curse that Alex's foster brother had tattooed into Shane's ankle had remained. The dark magic had left him in a state of perpetual internal bleeding and psychosis until Alex and Ryan teased it out and destroyed it.

"I'm not staying here to help you. In fact, I won't be any part of this. I won't be any part of you, either of you!" It wasn't him; he didn't mean it. I could keep telling myself those things, but I wasn't sure about the Demon influence. Had he made Jax feel that way permanently? Could one night erase all the years we had together? The Demon had threatened to ruin our lives and maybe this was his back-up plan all along. He used Jax's form to trick me, and then Jax was there and everything was falling apart.

"Keep away from me, both of you. I don't want to see either of you again after tonight, unless you can tell me I'm wrong. Tell me you didn't kill him." Jax saw the guilt in our eyes. I couldn't help it. I had never been in a situation like that before and we had no idea what to do or how to keep calm and fix everything that was going so terribly wrong.

"That's what I thought." With that, he turned away, leaving Logan and me in the rain with a dead body and our suffering. Grief struck us both at the realization that even though we still lived and breathed, we had lost our lives. The very lives that Logan had sacrificed everything to save.

CHAPTER 7

Time

Logan had killed a man. No, let me rephrase. *We* had killed a man, because, yes, I blamed myself for my role and my mistake. Staying put may have saved the man, at least that is my belief—one that has been haunting me for years.

With the car windows down I breathe in the saltwater air, trying my hardest to cleanse my mind of the painful memories. Warm breeze moves through my hair and, once I surface from the Hampton Roads Tunnel, my tension eases. While I cross the bridge, darkness falls around me, the moon's glow reflects bright crests of waves in the bay, and casts an otherworldly glow in all directions. I knew I wouldn't be able to come back here without combing through the whole story again. Logan and I will have to relive it together, as well, if we are ever to have a hope of moving on.

I was torn when Jax disappeared from that horrifying scene. There was no way I could leave Logan to deal with the poor unfortunate soul at our feet, but Jax had been cursed to believe a Demon's lies, and he needed a remedy. All I wanted was for him to get help, for his sake and for the sake of our love. We never thought that we wouldn't be together forever. We'd loved each other since we were kids and nothing was going to keep us apart.

Logan moved quickly into problem-solving mode and called our aunt Aime as soon as we tore out of the storage area in his all-wheel drive Audi. I could hear Aime's voice through the phone, and even though some of her tones went into some of the higher note ranges, she was calm and gave him specific instructions. We drove into the night, away from Blacksburg, Virginia Tech, and Jax. Aime promised to call in a Healer right away to help Jax, but not being with him felt wrong to me.

We met John, an Earthen Protector, in a desolate mountain area near Charlottesville. I was deeply disappointed that it wasn't Alana, feeling that she was the only one who could help us out of this mess. Yet John was quiet and efficient. The body was removed from our world, instantly, but with an intense amount of effort from his Earthen magic. John wasn't much older than us, late twenties. He had a rich, Nigerian accent, and his skin nearly disappeared into the night. He was accompanied by a Healer named Corinne, and the two were night and day. Corinne glowed next to him with her pale, moonlight skin, fiery red hair, and large green eyes. Despite their looks they worked in unison, tandem beings complementing each other. I wondered if they were in love, in love like Jax and I. The thought brought me to tears while her hands roved over me, seeping cold tendrils into my being that gave me surprising comfort and brought calm to my tremors. She eyed me compassionately before trying to speak.

"I'm fine," I lied, interrupting her. "It's my brother and Jax I'm worried about."

"My sister, Nina, is helping Jax. He's in good hands, I promise you." Corinne gave my arm a squeeze and smiled at me before moving to Logan. Worry creased her brow when she took in the state of his clothing and the tattooed bird on his arm. When her fingers brushed his painted skin, the bird moved and I swear he sighed. It had been a long night for all of us. She moved to whisper to John, and they spoke in hushed tones with their backs to us.

"Whatever you have to say, say it to us. We're the ones who fought the Demon and we're the ones living with the price, so at least give us the courtesy of being straight with us." Logan's demeanor was calm but intense, reflecting pure strength. For a moment, I thought everything would be okay. I mean, if he was keeping it together then we had a chance.

John and Corinne turned to us and nodded in agreement. "The Demon's energy was obvious in the man's body. You shouldn't blame yourselves for what happened. It's an ongoing war and you two were pulled into it very young. However, we feel it's best that you keep your heads down for a while, at least until things cool down. John will return to Blacksburg and take care of any evidence at the scene. You two return, act normal, and don't discuss what happened with anyone. Nothing should change, for now." My insides began to twist, creating a sickening feeling. Would everything be normal with Jax? I eyed Logan's arm and wondered how normal Logan could possibly be.

"What about the Nanda-yi? Is it safe for Logan to have it, basically, attached to him?" Logan's face snapped toward me quick as a whip and I shied from him, for the first time in my life almost fearful of my brother. Regret and sadness flitted over his features and I knew my reaction had wounded him. He probably thought it was because of the dead man, but it wasn't, I knew that had been an accident. Logan would never have killed an innocent person, never. No, my fear was of the eagle and its unknown impact on my Logan. Just as I was about to let him know all of that, John spoke to us.

"The Nanda-yi has chosen its Seer, having found him worthy, and only Logan can remove him and return him to his wooden domain. Logan will need to train with him and learn to not only control, but also to work with the Nanda-yi. I believe that any harm caused previously is now over, as the bird seems at peace. Logan, we have an idea of where you can get the most help, if you'll accept it. It'll mean turning over your life to the training, but you'd be making a real difference in the world." Logan latched onto the idea; I knew he wanted to make up for what he had done, but I selfishly didn't want him away from me again. The last time we were apart, things spun out of control and that was where we now were, scattered, changed, and I feared things would never be the same. But Logan nodded and John walked with him to speak of the possibility of the new life that awaited.

"Things aren't ever going to be the same for Logan—for us—are they?" Corrine looked at me and placed her hands on my shoulders, her touch bringing them some much-needed relaxation.

"No, Sandra, death and Demons cause chaos, but that doesn't mean the change will be all bad or that it will last forever. Go back to school, graduate, and then each of you will have to decide what happens next. You and Logan need time to heal, and hopefully Jax's curse will be lifted soon without having caused irreparable harm. Emotions and memories are strong despite Demon tampering, so give him time."

Logan and I left when the sun had begun its slow rise, bringing life and light to the world. The Blue Ridge Mountains' beauty and vastness usually made me smile, but not today. Their massive presence was almost unbearable, as if they were staring down at us in judgment. Each cloud molded itself into a face of mistrust and disappointment, making me close my eyes in hopes of escaping the torment. Logan, thankfully at first, distracted me. I quickly came to realize that I might have rather dealt with the faces in the sky than hear what he had to say. He told me about John's offer to take him to the FBI academy in Quantico where he would be trained and molded into a Special Agent. John felt Logan could do a lot of good in preventing worldwide acts of evil and catastrophe, especially now that he had the Nanda-yi. It wasn't far, not far at all, but he would be off the grid for a while; no one could call in and he wouldn't be able to call out. After all that had happened, I didn't want to believe that I wouldn't be able to see or talk to my brother.

"Just during your training, right? Won't you get some free passes or something?" I was getting choked up thinking about it. He had only recently joined us at school, and I had been able to see him every day. Logan looked uncertain.

"Even after my training at the academy is complete, I think it's best that we continue to lay low for a while. I've done

77

nothing but bring evil into our lives, failing again and again when you've always known, and I never listened."

"That's not true! We made our decisions together. It's not anyone's fault! We take the blame for this together." The Demon was right; my world was falling apart and he was responsible. Hatred boiled in my stomach and I only wished to see his existence end. Logan had been my best friend since birth, and I could feel my deep connection with him slipping away. His face was wearing that stoic, my-mind's-made-up look and I cried quietly within my soul.

"I see the fear in your eyes when you look at me now. You're afraid of me. Hell, maybe you should be." I shook my head, which served two purposes. One, to tell myself not to cry, and two, to show him how ridiculously asinine he was being.

"No! No, that's not it. I'm worried about that bird. About what he may do to you or how he might change you. That's all. I love you, Logan. You're my best friend. Mom and Dad are gone; it's you and me, remember?" His face fell for a moment and then immoveable Logan reappeared.

"It's for the best, Sandra. Maybe when things calm down, and we know for sure that what we've done won't come back to haunt us, we can bring things back to where they were. But for now I need to leave. Maybe you should too. You always wanted to move out west, why not now? Leave what happened here behind you." I couldn't believe what was happening. Less than forty-eight hours ago that would have never crossed our minds, and now our lives had been tossed up in the air to twist and turn before landing on the board haphazardly and deciding our lives.

"What about Jax? You're going to abandon him, too?" He flinched and I knew I'd wounded him with my choice of words.

"I'm not abandoning either of you. This is for the best. Jax will be fine, in time. He's always loved you, Sandra; he won't ever leave you." I thought Logan would never leave me either, but there we were, saying good-bye.

We rode in silence for most of the trip back to Virginia Tech. He dropped me off at my apartment and we hugged in the absence of words. I touched his arm one last time, touching the bird on his stunning head and looking deep into his eyes. I used my mind to send the bird images of my life with Logan, showing the Nanda-yi I loved him, and begging him to keep him safe. I swear he nodded at me before going still and distant. The goodbye tore a piece of my heart away, but it was only one way that the Demon destroyed my life as I had known it.

I showered and changed before booking it to Jax's studio apartment. Maybe if I looked totally different from the last time he saw me, the feelings of betrayal and disgust wouldn't surface. Nina answered the door when I arrived. She had Corrine's eyes and ivory skin, but her hair was midnight black, long, and wavy. If I were to picture a twenty-first-century witch in my mind, Nina would be my template. I could smell the spent power on her, as well as see the exhaustion in her eyes, and I knew before she spoke a word that Jax wasn't back to normal, and that perhaps he never would be.

"Physically, Jax is in perfect health. However, I can't completely lift the curse without altering pieces of him, his memories, personality . . . emotions. That Demon did a number on him.

At first, I believed I'd removed most of it. He does seem to find clarity for a while, which is when he calls for you, but then he's pulled back into the same cursed reality. I'm sorry, Sandra. I think with more work, time, and maybe a dead Demon, he will return to normal. My sister and I will rotate, as will one more of us. We'll do whatever we can, I promise." That was the break in the dam for me. My sobs wouldn't stop as I cried for Jax, Logan, the dead man who had no chance of returning to those he loved, and for myself.

Nina tried to touch me, but I flinched away from her, disgusted with myself. "Maybe this would always have been the case, Demon curse or not. We lied to him and made a very dangerous decision without trusting him to help us. And then what does he stumble into? Logan and I covering up a . . ." Nina shushed me and moved closer. Even her shush was calming, damn it.

"Corrine and John told you not to speak of what happened. You can't risk having attention put on you or brought to our kind. We work in this world with powers that normal people would never understand, especially not a court of law, should it come to that. Best to forget it happened, and take some time away from each other till it all blows over. I can aid you, should you need my services."

"No, thank you, I'll live with this burden. If I'm going to lose everyone I love, than I sure as hell better remember why." Nina allowed me to hang around for when Jax's mind was clear. I thought it was what I wanted, but after having those blissful minutes and then reliving his feelings of disappointment and ire, I regretted the decision. Nina had to shut him down before he told the entire apartment complex what we had done. No matter what was happening to him, there was no way I would ever believe that he would turn on us or report us, but Nina and her Healer sisters would make sure. Without a kiss goodbye, and with him urging me to leave and never come back, I closed Jax's door. My body felt heavier than it had ever felt before, and I leaned in to rest my head against the door's strong wood and endless memories. Saying a prayer to Gaia, I asked her to heal my love and to bring him back to me, and then, then I took the hardest steps of my life, and left.

Leaving the apartment that minute led to days of no contact with either Jax or Logan, aside from graduation where Logan and I sat next to each other. Jax wasn't there.

In what felt like a blink of my eye, I was saying goodbye to Logan. When he walked to his door, he turned and told me he loved me, but he also told me something I would never forget.

"Sandra, I meant what I said; you should go out west. Forget about what happened here, and forget Jax and me for a while. You don't need to check up, call, or visit. You really don't and you really shouldn't. Do you understand?"

"For how long? What if he needs me? What if I can help?" I was tired of crying, but I couldn't help or stop the tears from rolling down my cheeks. It felt as if Logan was banishing me like some Demon.

"I'm trying to keep you safe, Sandra, like I always do. Now listen to me and leave. Don't come back or contact me unless it's an emergency. Do you understand? I love you. I have to go."

And with that, Logan was gone from my life for what I thought would be mere months, but which turned to years. I went back to Jax's place. The other Healer was there, the one I hadn't met. Her dark skin and beautiful lips had shocked me then, but even more now as I work through these torturous memories. Those eyes had flashed across Jax's phone screen earlier today and I hadn't recognized her. Years of forced forgetting can do that to a person. The third Healer is Jax's other woman, the one he is considering taking the next step with. Part of me simmers with mistrust, wondering if she got close to him by happenstance while trying to heal him, or if she managed to keep him away from me for her own gain. Damn, jealousy hasn't flamed within me for a long time but here she is, Rhonda Rousey-style, in stilettos, cracking her knuckles and looking for a fight.

My thoughts cycle back and forth between calling him and calling Corinne or Nina. Would they even tell me the truth? Maybe they were all in on it, and maybe not. Jax is amazing and if she fell for him, I wouldn't be surprised. And if he spent years loathing me, why wouldn't he fall for the gorgeous Healer girl?

Back then, I did get one last moment with him before I left for the west coast, and that time I didn't linger long enough for his venom to reappear. I knew he was returning to Sandbridge, at least for the summer, and I, I left for San Diego, doing my damnedest to not look back.

CHAPTER 8

Sandbridge

Duke Dumont's 'Ocean Drive' echoes through the speakers of the slick driving machine. The music curls through my body, calming my emotions and easing the stress of my memories.

The winding road to Sandbridge is dark and soothing. Waterbirds fish, and a heron standing frozen on one leg eagerly awaits its dinner. The Lotus Garden Park lights up under my headlights, showing me the giant lily pads with their blooms stretching toward the moonlight. A magic path can almost be seen from the blossoms to the bright orb in the night sky, and I decelerate to enjoy the view. Insects chitter and chirp in time with Duke's lyrics and my foot hits the accelerator again, moving me quickly toward my home. As I turn right onto Sandfiddler Road—our road—the lyrics weave inside me, causing my heart to beat faster with excitement.

Our house comes into view, a soft glow lighting the three-story rectangular window and revealing the long wooden staircase that leads to all levels. Memories of Jax looking through that window after he'd walked me home, watching every step I took, brings warmth to my cheeks. I always knew he was watching and worked to make my moves more graceful and my shy smile more intriguing each time I turned his way. Once, he chased me up those stairs when my parents were away and we fell onto the last landing in a heap of warm touches and passionate kisses. That was the first night we made love.

I pull into the driveway and look affectionately at the soft blues and whites of the wooden exterior. Childhood memories make me smile. 'Ocean Drive' has turned my mood around, the sexy electronic beats pushing out any bad memories of Jax under the Demon's influence, and replacing them with better ones, ones that warm me. I hurry inside and go immediately to the back porch. The sound of the ocean waves hits me like a pleasant hand touching my heart and I breathe in the eastern shore's sights, sounds, and scents. My ears listen to the ebb and flow of the waves crashing and retreating. Their watery movement is different than the West coast, neither better nor worse than the other—just different. One reminds me of home, while the other is my place of healing and escape.

The next few minutes entail me slipping into a short, sheer beach dress, turning on the stereo throughout the house speakers, and giving myself a long pour of wine. I walk back outside, swaying to the sounds of both the sea and the throbbing beats from the speakers. A hawk dives from high heights into the sea before reclaiming the sky with a struggling fish in its claws. I shiver along my spine, thinking momentarily about being like that fish, caught in the Demon's claws that night in the sheets of pouring rain. I take a long sip of the dark Zin, which tantalizes my tongue before its velvety smoothness slips down my throat, soothing my momentary queasiness.

Morgan Page comes over the radio. In my mind's eye I picture his boyish cheeks and full lips, ever the gentlemen, when he spun at Rapture last month. I danced all night next to him in the DJ booth, pouring my heart into my movements during one of his newest tracks, 'Running Wild.' Now, here is the same voice calling to me in the night. When my thoughts turn to the love of my life's face and delicious lips, my sensuality reaches boiling point—Jax.

My mind and soul beg for Jax, for his hands on my skin, his lips on my throat. My hands travel my body in the warm night air. I grip the bottom of my dress, revealing my legs to the edges of my lace panties. As if on cue, soft hands replace mine on my thigh, and what I first thought was wishful thinking or a night dream becomes reality when I open my eyes to see him next to me. What? Is he really here? I reach out and feel his skin under my fingertips. Yes, he is real and here, here with me on this night.

"How did you know I was . . ." His lips cover mine and I decide not to care.

"Why didn't you call me, Sandra? I know you want to be with me; it's what I want, too." I can't even think while his warm hands move from the outside of my hips to my inner thighs. I clench inside as I feel warmth from my belly traveling down, heating the soft spots between my legs.

"Oh, Jax, I've missed you." I don't care about what Logan said or about the Healer girl on Jax's phone. Jax is mine. I deserve him. He has always been mine and I want him. Right now. Morgan's beats allow the lyrics to break through and I sway against Jax who is still positioned behind me. While one hand squeezes and caresses my inner thigh, the other runs up my belly to cover my breast. I heave into the touch of his hand, soft, but strong and full of his need for me.

> *I never did belong, tomorrow I'll be gone. Don't cry, momma, don't cry. I'm burning down this town. So if you see me 'round tonight. Kiss me goodbye.*

> *I'm running wild, I'm getting free, I'm running wild, I'm running, you are next to me.*

"Why did I ever let you leave?" he says, nuzzling my neck. "It feels like a bad dream that you've been gone so long. I want to make it up to you." Goddess, yes! He can make it up to me right now.

"Jax, I love you." I spin around and kiss him hard. My lips are tingling with passion and I use my tongue to tease him one second while my teeth nibble on his bottom lip the next. A growl forms in his chest while his hand moves from my inner thigh to the underside of my knee. He lifts my leg and positions it on one of the chaise lounge chairs. Dropping to his knees in front of me, he lifts my dress completely, eyeing my lace panties then looking up at me with an expression of want and lust that makes me moan. Fingers tickle up my leg and yank on one side of the lace garment. His finger takes hold of the fabric, twisting it and causing it to press against my clitoris as he pulls on it slightly. A warm knuckle brushes my spot softly, dragging another moan from my lips and my hand to his hair. I arch back just before warm air touches my inner thigh followed by his kisses along my sensitive skin toward his bound finger. I feel movement, knowing I am exposed fully before he slips his tongue inside.

"Oh, Jax!" It comes out in a deep, throbbing moan. I vaguely remember that we are outside and sound travels wicked fast in the dunes of the oceanside. The wetness he creates is overwhelming, his mouth nearly driving me to climax instantly. His fingers slip in next, first one, two, and then three. He moves them softly at first, but as I push against him roughly he responds by driving them in deeper and faster. My legs start to shake and I wonder how much longer I can handle him not being fully inside me. Tongue replaces fingers and I am wild with need as his hot, wet, slick fingers roam teasingly around my backside.

He lifts me suddenly and lays me back onto the chaise, kneeling before me again to continue tasting my flesh. His fingers and tongue work together and all I can do is grip his shoulder and the chair, crying out with pleasure and pain as I climax in time with the breaking waves. As if he weren't turned on before, my peak has sent him into a frenzy. He roams his mouth all over me, up my belly, stopping to press himself into my breasts and tease my hardened nipples. One hand stays down to continually ravish me, but now he is in range so I can do the same for him.

With my hands on his chest, I force him to lift up enough so I can pull his shirt over his head and work his jeans and boxers to the porch floor. My eyes linger on his gloriously hard, sculptured torso. Goddess, this man is in shape. I can't keep my hands off him. My attention is quickly drawn to his hard cock when its warmth and soft skin glides along my belly. I pull him higher, getting him right between my breasts, lifting slightly to get his tip close to my mouth so my lips can touch him, making him wet, and somehow even harder, instantly. When I push him back down to my breasts, I squeeze them while he rocks into me. I continue to flick my tongue on his cock's tip over and over again, licking him, and my fingers, to keep the action slippery and hot. Jax looks into my eyes and passion takes me over. I squeeze him between my hips and flip us over. After wiggling out of my panties, I straddle him while gripping the back of the chaise. Reaching behind me, I guide him so that he can enter me, which he does, slowly at first, teasing me with his tip before driving into me fully.

"Baby, I want you to moan. Oh, Sandra. Baby, you're the best. I've missed you so much." Jax's gasping words of love, of lust, of having missed me, drive me crazy with need. My hands grip his shoulders and I clench down hard while rocking on top of him hard and fast. Jax grips my waist roughly and pulls himself up slightly to take my breast into his mouth, biting down on my nipple, and sucking on it tenderly one moment and rough the next. I feel him harden and expand inside me, causing me to arch back and circle my hips aggressively, grinding against him as we both near our sensual peaks.

Love engulfs me when wave after wave of painfully pleasurable release rocks us both. I fall against him while he wraps his strong, warm arms around me with a promise to never let me go falling from his lips. We lie there, spent, enjoying each other's comfort and placing light, feathery, soft kisses on each other's lips. How have I been without this man for so long? How did I stay away?

"Never again." I whisper to him. He doesn't need to think about what I mean; he feels it just as I do.

"No, Sandra. We'll never be apart ever again." He lifts both of us easily and walks slowly into the house. Once in my bedroom, he heads to the bathroom, turning on the shower and pulling me into the warm water next to him. We caress and wash each other with equal motions of love and adoration. I lean against him in the water and allow the suds to drip down my back and slip along my legs. This is where I am supposed to be, in his arms, safe and happy.

After drying off and lazily getting dressed, we lie on the bed nibbling on cheese, fruit, and breads. We laugh out loud, reliving memories of our lives together, from escapades as children, to the first kiss he stole from me, to making love in this very bed. At some point we have to face what has kept us apart for so long, so I break into our perfect world of memory lane to ask.

"What changed, Jax? After all these years, even with the Healers' help, why are you able to forgive me now?" His face drops the smile that has been plastered there for the last hour, and concern shadows his features.

"I can't really explain, truly. But about a week ago my mind cleared; I found myself wondering where you were and how in the world I ever let you leave. I was scrambling to make sense of everything. I'd had moments of clarity before, only to have them disappear and be replaced by what I can only describe as someone else's thoughts, someone else's feelings, rage. I've had patients with acute psychotic breaks who have described to me what it felt like. They said it was like being locked inside their own minds, fighting to make their bodies and words respond to what they were really feeling, but instead watching in horror as something else took over. That's what it felt like to me."

"The Demon," I whisper, feeling an icy chill run from my neck down along my arms at the memory of the Demon's hands on me.

"Yes, the Demon. Before, I couldn't listen, but when my mind cleared, about a week ago, Mya told me everything." Ah, that's who she is: The beautiful Healer goddess on his phone. "She let me know how I'd been tricked, and what you and Logan went through that night. I'm so sorry, Sandra. I thought I was stronger than that . . ." I touch his cheek, feeling that even his despair looks strong on him. I kiss him and then try to help us both heal.

"Everyone told me to give you time, and Logan told me to lay low, and to basically stay away from both of you. I was so hurt and confused, but I was also powerless. Logan was always more of the leader, as you know, but time, and my friends in San Diego, has changed a lot of things for me. I'll never be pushed away again. I should have fought for you then, or at the very least, come back before now."

"I'm not sure you would have liked what you came back to. My personal life had been shattered so I dove into med school and then work. I was like a robot. I made very few friends and lots of enemies and plenty of competition. The Demon's curse changed me, as did your absence, but I'm grateful to the Healers. Once they knew the curse had lifted they all—Mya,

Nina, Corinne—helped bring me all the way back to the man I was before—to the man that loves you." He squeezes me closer to him before continuing. "I used my Sight just in time to see you coming the following day. It was all a blur, but I steeled myself to meet you, and just hoped for the best."

"Well, what about Mya? I don't want to come between you and someone who's cared for you so much after Logan and I abandoned you." Jax shakes his head and bends to kiss my shoulder.

"I think she knew that when I came back my heart would go right to you. There's no way that shell of a man would have been good for her, and I think deep down she knew I wasn't nearly the man she needed to make her happy. Every time I managed to come out of the curse I spoke about you. It wouldn't have been fair to her, so I'm glad we never became more than good friends." My inner cheerleader brushes her brow with that close call and does a back flip, her pom-poms spazzing in response.

"I want to thank her. She helped bring you back to me, even though she has feelings for you. It's the least I can do." He nods and then looks questioningly at me.

"Why did you marry someone else? Did you do it to punish me?"

Man, that's a stake through the heart.

"No, Goddess, it was more like punishing myself. I felt I was to blame for everything. If I'd stayed put maybe that man would still be alive. If I'd just gone against Logan, and instead told you about his visions and fears, maybe you would never have been tricked by that Demon. That awful regret made me reckless and desperate, and that's when I met Drew." My eyes are welling up now, damn it. I will not cry.

"Sandra, it wasn't your fault. We were fooling ourselves in college, thinking we were safe from the evils our parents had faced. I knew, as well as you did, that Logan transferring to Tech was odd, and I should've made him tell me why. I'm at fault as much as Logan. We should have carried the burden together—not scattered." He is right about Logan, but I won't blame Jax one bit. He was used as a pawn and our love suffered because of it.

"I feel terrible about my marriage. You're the only man I ever saw myself with. I don't know what I was doing. I felt orphaned, abandoned by my only sibling, and feeling that I'd lost the only man I'd ever truly love. That Demon turned me into a vulnerable idiot. I trusted Drew to at least take care of me—I had no one else. I was lost there for a while, but the good news is that after getting out of that travesty of a marriage, I got back to myself, to the Sandra I hadn't been since I lost you and Logan—even more so, in fact. I have powerfully gifted friends who are like family now, and I do work that I love. My Seer abilities have helped save people and fight Demons." Well, we may have actually befriended one, but now isn't quite the time to bring that up. "And now, now that I have you back in my life—hopefully Logan as well—I don't want to look back, at least not for us. Logan and I still have to face off so I can earn his help, but you and me, can we be, just be from now on?"

He smiles and kisses me. "You're my love, Sandra, my one true love. My heart is yours and I'm happy to let go of the painful stuff. Logan and I need to bury some of our own demons, as well. The Nanda-yi was important to me; it chose me, but it also chose him. Perhaps I received the totem in the first place so that eventually I could lead him to Logan—his rightful owner. If he's making the world a better place, then it's meant to be." Jax is really back, the strong, amazing boy I fell in love with years ago. My home is relaxing us and binding us together again. I'm not going to worry about what will happen next, how we will make this work, because we will and that is all that matters.

"I'm really happy things are going well in San Diego, Sandra," he continues. "I'm glad that Logan and I didn't stop you from living your life and finding happiness. I wouldn't be able to live with myself if that were true." Well, besides marrying that first-class cheating asshole Drew, having to walk in on a kinky weird-ass threesome in our bedroom, topped with the fact that Alex is who knows where, I have been happy in my work and friendships. My love life, on the other hand, although interesting, meant nothing to me—I thought I would never have Jax again, and nobody would ever be good enough to take his place.

"Well, it hasn't all been good; I was broken for a while. Not anymore, though. You're my missing piece, Jax. You've always had my heart and I don't ever, ever, ever want to lose you again."

He kisses me deeply and the need to feel him inside me again flares to life. Still in each other's arms, we reclaim our lost time together, and promise, amidst kisses, caresses, and words of love, to never let go again.

CHAPTER 9

Nanda-yi

Not this vision again. My hands are bloody, and no, I won't look down. I can't bear to see Jax dying by my hands. A strong hand grabs my right shoulder and I turn to see Jax looking at me reassuringly. Another touch on my left, and there is Logan; he too looks at me with support and comfort. With them by my side, I take a chance and look down. The man from our past is lying there, dead in the rain. Tears run down my cheeks. He opens his eyes, locking onto mine. "I forgive you," he says.

I wake to the sounds of waves crashing and, I swear, the smell of pancakes and bacon. The dream crawls over me and I feel wet from the rain even though I am warm and dry in bed. Whatever that was, I have hope for today. Perhaps old wounds will be healed; perhaps the old vision of Jax dead was my own fear that he would never forgive me and that it was our love that was dead. Well, I think last night proved that wrong!

With tingling reminders from last night brushing away my worries, I leap out of bed and run into the kitchen, only a blanket wrapped around my body. It is still as warm as last night, the Virginia weather failing to drop in temp in the evenings like the cooler San Diego nights. A foil-covered plate is on the counter next to a note that merely says:

Surfing. I love you.

He mustn't have been gone long since the goodies inside are warm, as is the syrup he left in a mug next to my plate. I move outside to sit and eat where I can watch him in the waves. It doesn't take long for him to sense me and wave in my direction. I could get used to this. I hope Jax will come with me to San Diego, but we would also have to make sure to spend time right here. Would he move his practice for me, or would he expect me to move back here? What is most important, now that I know we will be together, whatever the case, is to get Logan on board with the Alex-finding mission. He is going to need to come with me to San Diego. I hope Jax can just take some time off for now and join us. All the other pieces can fall nicely into place later.

I suddenly feel a wave of nausea. What if this is another Demon trick to tear me apart again? Could that monster possibly have known that I was coming back, and relieve Jax's curse at just the right time only to rip him away from me again? No, no that can't be true. Logan would have known and warned me, wouldn't he? I have to believe it. Plus, last night I saw nothing remaining of the darkness that claimed Jax years ago. He is my Jax and I am going to stay positive about what appears to be a well-timed miracle.

I continue eating and watching him in the distance. Despite

my assumption that he hadn't been surfing at all lately, it is either old hat to him, or my assessment was wrong. The sun's glow is beautiful on the blue water and the dunes' tall grasses wave at me from their sandy homes. It is going to be a hot day; sweat is already forming on my brow and between my breasts where my blanket is firmly secured. I abandon my plate to return inside for a bikini and some sunscreen. It is early, but I am already feeling the intensity of the rays on my cheeks.

Grabbing a hat before heading back outside, I freeze when I hear a car turn into the driveway. Damn, it's Logan. My pristine morning and post-best-fuck-ever mood is going down the drain quickly. Hell, I'm not going to take no for an answer, or have him treat me like he's in charge. No, we are the same age, damn it! Okay, so he's a couple minutes older but that just made him pushy. Alex and the thought of Avalon have piqued his interest, so I need to ride it out. We aren't in danger, the years have passed, and we have never been questioned about that night. I never even googled it, and I ignored topics or whispers that might have led to digging for information about the man we killed. We are safe. Logan and Jax should be able to repair their friendship as well, and once we are all back on even ground, we can go save Alex. Yay us! So why do I still feel so sick?

I snag a beach cover-up and walk back outside, deciding to appear unruffled by his presence. Jax continues to surf, oblivious to Logan's arrival. Turning to stress eating, I dig into my plate and devour the salty meat and sweet, syrup-covered cake. No need to bicker on an empty stomach. Plus, he did say emergencies were okay reasons to break the silence, and this is a damn emergency.

"I'd have to agree with you on that one, girlie. Let's get this show on the road so I can get the hell out of wherever 'here' is."

She's back. Alex is awake and coherent. This is a much better time and place to let Logan in on the connection I have with her, so much better than doing it at Quantico, when I might have looked like a complete lunatic.

"I have one hell of a headache, but I think I remembered something. Justin is dead, isn't he? I remember that and I also remember the anger and hell to pay right afterwards. Was that a coincidence? Did it have something to do with him dying? I can't even guess anymore with all the Demons, Absolute Protectors, Avalon, Healers, Seers. It's all a clusterfuck, if you ask me!"

She is surly, which is a good sign . . . I hope. I feel her sadness about Justin. He loved her and I know she cared for him strongly. Maybe not as much as he wanted or needed her to, and as a result, he went off the deep end.

"Hold on there, girl. Logan's here and we're going to get into our visions of what happened surrounding your disappearance. Do you remember anything about the night you left for Montana? Anything about Justin?"

"Montana? What? Damn it, Sandra, right now I don't even remember going there. Wait, we . . . we who? Damn it, we fought something vicious somewhere I've been before. I know that much. I'm still spent from it all." The woman killed a Demon not even a week ago and she can't remember a thing. Shit. Oh my god, wait . . . she killed a Demon around the same time that Jax came out of his curse. Are they related? Could it be that Alex's father's Demon was our Demon? Did Alex save Jax? Did she save the love of my life?

Before I can continue this OMG moment, Logan is at the

doorway to the balcony, looking at me curiously, wondering about my sanity, I am sure.

"I see Jax is here. I thought I made myself clear about him. You do know he works with the Seer's Order, don't you? He could be here for us."

"Ease up, Logan. We were cleared by Corrine and John that night. Why would the Seer leadership be after us?" He glares at me, crossing his arms and grinding his teeth. Hoping to spare us time before a full-on Logan and Jax reunion, I move inside.

"What about me, Sandra? I misused my Sight repeatedly. Don't you think they may have something to say about that?" I roll my eyes, probably not the best idea but I am so sick of living with his paranoia. It used to seep into me and take me over as well. I would have thought he'd outgrown it by now, but I'm not the one who struck the final blow, and I don't know if Logan can ever get over what he did to that poor soul. I walk toward him with my hands raised in a placating manner, smiling, and trying to play the calming sister just like I always have.

"Look, Logan. You have to forgive yourself. We all need to move past the mistakes of that night. You're a good person. You help the world every day. Don't you feel as though you've paid your dues?"

"I can help him forget. Look at his tan, look at those muscular arms. Dang, I hope you convince him to save me, Sandra. What? Too much?" For Goddess' sakes, Alex! She certainly has a knack for timing.

"He had a wife and a child. Did you know that? They'll never know what happened to him, maybe never believe he's really dead. Can you imagine living like that? Not knowing if the person you love is alive and lost, or dead?"

Damn, couldn't we have found a way to put these people at ease? Why didn't a Healer get called in? "Maybe we can think of a way to give them peace?"

"I've asked and been told to stay away from the whole thing. Humans heal, was all they kept telling me. The government can be unfeeling at times." Now that I can believe.

"Well, I know some people who I think can help. One is high up in the Earthen Protector Council; I'm sure he would help us. And the other, well, that's who I need your help bringing back." Ryan will definitely help if it's at all possible. Even more so if we can bring Alex back to him.

"Logan," I go on, "I promise to try and help that poor man's family, I really do, but I have something urgent to tell you. My friend—Alex—she's communicating with me right now. Can you help me find her? We need to get her out of wherever she is, and *now*." His head cocks to the side, like he is trying to look into my mind. As if on cue, his war bird dislodges from the tattoo ink, instead becoming all flesh and wicked claws gripping onto Logan's arm. The raptor reaches his strong neck toward me and I meet beady, yet gentle eyes. Logan speaks out loud, but not to me.

"Alex? Alex, can you hear me?" The bird turns toward Logan and shocks the shit out of me by opening his beak and spilling out Alex's voice.

"Nice to meet you, Logan. I can see why Sandra kept you hidden from me, or is it because you're naughty? That's not a deal breaker, I assure you." Yes, that damn bird begins to look Logan up and down hungrily and I muffle a guffaw at his astonishment.

He looks at me. "Is she always like this or do you think she's been drugged or cursed?"

"Oh, I've definitely been put under something," Alex's voice replies, "though not something as fun as you, I'm sure." The bird winks this time and I can't help the hand that smacks my forehead and slides down my face.

"Alex, darling? Will you be serious for a moment? Logan is trying to help us. Can you describe what's around you, before you drift off again? Is there anything you can remember that will help us find who took you?"

"He took me, silly."

"Who, Alex? A Demon? Who? Are you in Avalon?" Maybe Logan is right; she appears to be very loopy.

"Justin . . . his spirit took me and I'm paying for my crimes. Maybe I'm dead and this is just my spirit haunting you. OOOOO." The bird's head droops and then begins to look around frantically. "Someone's coming. Oh, Sandra, please get me out of here. I keep forgetting. What if I forget you and I lose this connection between us? Help me! Please! Promise me you'll look into the visions of what happened before I left for wherever it was you said I went and fought that fucking beast from hell. It has to help you find me. That's the black hole in my memory. Oh god, who's that?" The Nanda-yi lets out a screech so terrifying that the glass windows shake and dishes clatter in their cabinets. Logan and I instinctively drop to the ground, shielding our heads and moving close together. When the noise clears, the connection to Alex has gone and Jax is hauling ass toward the house.

The Nanda-yi hops on to the floor next, shaking his body before his head whips around toward Jax. Letting out a powerful yet this time joyful screech in his direction I'm reminded of those dog and owner reunion videos on the Internet. Jax skids to a halt and smiles at the eagle. When he continues walking toward us, his steps are lighter, no longer afraid once he sees Logan and me together, and safe. The eagle's face reaches toward Logan's for a moment and, once getting a nod from my brother, he lifts off the tile floor, flying toward the back door. I move into motion and open the door, allowing the bird to fly to Jax. Without fear, Jax stretches out his arm where the eagle makes a graceful landing. Jax's eyes black over and calm settles all around us. I watch a tear streak down his cheek in the longest two minutes of my life. Once Jax's eyes clear he walks to the house and approaches the two of us. The Nanda-yi flaps his wings while Jax strokes his strong body. The bird nudges his strong, sharp beak on Jax's cheek and my little mental cheerleader shakes her head, wondering why I want her to give a "hooray" for the strange scene. She must be thinking 'lucky her' for ending up in my jacked-up mind and world. The eagle lifts himself into the air, returning to his normal resting place, merging his flesh into Logan's arm.

Jax is the first to speak, crossing the space between us to hug me before turning to Logan. "You saved us. The Nanda-yi showed me all your horrendous visions, all the scenarios that could have been if you hadn't done what you did that night. How did you live with those pictures in your mind? Sandra? Me? It must have been torture for you, and I haven't been there for you as a friend should be." Jax reaches out to Logan and grabs his shoulder. "You're like a brother to me, Logan. You should have never carried this burden alone for so long." In a rare moment, Logan's face softens and the two most important men in my life embrace. Tears of joy spring from my eyes and I give a silent thank you to the Goddesses of our world for bringing joy into the darkest places of my life.

What Logan says next makes an uncontrollable shudder roll through my body. "What worries me, looking back, is that I now believe that Demon was altering my visions to hide himself and the real reason for the Nanda-yi—so that he could possess it. The Nanda-yi gave me the feelings of dread-like warning in your apartment and then fought me tooth and nail once I got to the storage units. He shredded my chest, diving into my flesh over and over again before attaching to my arm. Honestly, I thought I was going to die." That explains his shirt. My growing nausea is making me thankful that I didn't take a closer look at it before Corrine used her healing powers. "Once the Nanda-yi realized I didn't know I was dealing with a Demon, and that I definitely had no intentions of giving him to a Demon, he worked with me instead of against me." I saw a proud, boyish smile on his face. The bird I once feared for him is obviously a good thing.

Jax breaks into Logan's story. "He was always supposed to go to you. He just showed me that in the visions. I kept him safe until you needed him. That I can accept." I revel in this moment of all of us being together. "He came to me for the sole purpose of finding his way to his rightful owner. You." Logan looks relieved. "I now know why you needed him and why you chose not to include me. My hope is that if I hadn't been cursed, I would have understood that right away and we wouldn't have had this distance between us for all these years. None of us could have controlled what happened that night, but at least you made sure Sandra was safe, and for that I owe you everything."

"Thanks, Jax. I've missed you both, and I know if the Demon hadn't gotten to you, things would have been different. I only wish I'd seen that coming and been able to prevent it." This bromance is something to behold, and makes me hopeful for our futures.

"I was able to do a lot of research on your totem, Jax. We know that Nanda-yi is an aboriginal word meaning "to see," but the eagle is also specifically the wedge-tailed eagle, or the persecuted and misunderstood king. A specific eagle who serves as a warning to people who use his power for evil, that they'll be destroyed. Many didn't and don't know that when the Nanda-yi was used, and people were hurt or killed, it was purely evil that he helped slay. Sometimes, yes, unfortunately, some innocents were possessed by evil. Learning all that was when I realized how close to death I'd been, at the bird's mercy." Logan rubs at his chest, I am sure remembering the pain and the close call he survived.

"Some stories I read painted the war eagle as an aggressor that others feared, not knowing that his victims were actually Demons, or possessed innocents, like in our case. The Demon sent me the visions of Sandra being taken and killed, and the bird knew that." Logan touches the painted feathers on his arm, taking a deep breath to settle his mind. "He thought I was possessed, or working with that "thing," but thankfully he saw the truth before he turned me to shreds."

"Why would he think you were there to do something evil? Couldn't he see that you were there to rescue me?"

Logan shakes his head at me before closing his eyes. "He also saw that I was going to kill a man, and he can't have known that the stranger was also possessed. I was the main target; I stole him and I was the one he felt was being controlled, which I was in a way. But I had to make a choice. It was either you or that man, Sandra. I saw the possible futures each time I looked into the vision. Sometimes I would tell both you and Jax, other times neither of you. In all versions, you were always the one in danger, but in other cases you both died." He turns his head to look at Jax, "It was madness, but Jax, I knew I had to leave you out of it. I'm glad you understand that now." Jax nods at him with sympathy in his eyes. Man, my man is hot when he cares!

"But I also knew the whole time that I was going to kill a man." I can see, by the tension in his strong face and clenching jaw, how hard this is for Logan to admit. "All I saw in the visions was a crazed man who wanted to kill either one or both of you, but with the Nanda-yi I was able to defeat him. After a while wondering who he was, an Absolute Protector or a crazed lunatic, I didn't care. All I cared about was keeping you both safe. So I did what I had to do with what I knew at the time." Jax's seemingly sentimental relic had once again taken over our lives, but that time Logan didn't refuse to take it, nor did he ignore the tingling warning the war bird gave him in his grasp. If he had, I might not be here today, and for that, my brother is a hero.

"I also learned more about you, Sandra." His words startle me and I start to worry about what else I am a part of in Loganland. "I reached out to Alana again—well, her name is Evie now. You may not realize what a talented Seer you are. Evie told me that you also have some Earthen Protector abilities. Not only can you use your powers to enter visions, but you can also move objects through space and time, much like the power Evie wields. You banished that Demon all by yourself, both times. You may not have known what you were doing, but you actually moved him through time to somewhere else. Out of the man's body, and then out of our world. I wish I'd known that before. Perhaps together we could have saved the man and killed the Demon instead."

My mind is spinning. Alex is a dimensional traveler and somehow I can move things through time and space? So, wait, can I bring her back myself? Whatever the case, I need to find her first. Time to fill the boys in on what I know, well, except the Demon killed Justin part for now. It's going to be bad enough when I tell them that another death happened on my watch. But it has to be done; Justin and his death may have something to do with her disappearance after all.

"Well, boys, I think now is a good time to bring the team back together. I have a friend in need and I think maybe we can be the ones to save her. After all, I'm pretty sure she took out our Demon. I mean, she did kill one a few days ago, and I doubt it's a coincidence that Logan is now free of the curse. Hmm? What do you guys think?" The looks on their faces are priceless, and confirmation enough for me. "Good. Now, let's pick our jaws up off the floor, boys, and go help out my girl."

CHAPTER 10

Unraveling

"Wait. Did I hear you correctly, Logan? You want us to let your bird 'tattoo' us? Hahaha, because that's what it sounded like the first three times you said it, but I must have heard you wrong, right?" Please say I am right, because I have not considered any more ink since the college right-of-passage tattoo on my ankle.

"Nope, sorry, Sis, you heard me right the first few times. Like I was saying, I think the Demon instilled in my visions that I had to *take* the Nanda-yi, not *ask* for it, and that I had to work alone or else you and Jax might both die. But now I believe that if we work together with the Nanda-yi, he'll make us all stronger. So, let's do just that. Getting the tattoos will make a strong bond for when we enter your visions, I'm sure of it. By the way, you can call my *bird* Yi. Easier, and he likes it." Logan looks at the bird and its sly eyes blink along with his quick, subtle head movements as if in agreement.

"You two communicate on a whole other level, don't you?" Jax is way too stoked about the eagle's tattoos we are about to get. Power sharing seemed all cute and kid-like when the three of us became blood brothers and sister, but this involves some pretty wild magic topped off with sharp-ass talons and a beak that can effortlessly shred a rabbit. Gulp. I am not a pussy, damn it, I just like my skin. And so does Jax. Instead of worrying, I eye his shirtless chest and ocean-styled hair. Maybe if I could have a few minutes alone with him my anxiety would ease up a tad.

Jax feels my hungry eyes on him and slides over to me. "Something I can help you with, darling?" Logan throws his hands in the air and lets out an exasperated sigh.

"Alex, people! Sandra, remember your friend? Geez, you two act like you haven't seen . . ." He stops, most likely due to the nasty glare I am shooting his way along with my "and what of it?" head tilt. But he is right. Time to get into the visions of my past with Alex and find out what was said and what the hell happened. After that, I hope to get my ass to wherever she is and bring her home.

My phone chimes on the counter. It's a text from Dana asking how things are going and when I am coming back. Oh, and that's not all, the Demon wants to know if I'm done *fucking* around. Delete delete delete! I have an entire and very public plane ride to San Diego when I can drop that Valant bombshell, so for now I'll just send a very polite response.

Leaving tonight or early A.M. so piss off—not you Dana, that's for V.

"Okay, now where were we? Oh yes, flesh maiming and then we head back to the night Alex left for Montana to kill the Demon." Logan nods and leads us into the living room. Jax eyes me when I loosen the tie on my cover-up, revealing more of my bikini, all for the sake of easy claw access. I'm so helpful.

"Jax would *love* to go first, Logan." Ouch, pinching is not nice. "What? You would. You're like a giddy schoolboy." My fingers touch his chest and I lean in to whisper to him. "A very strong and well-endowed schoolboy."

"Anything for you, baby. You know I like a little pain." Damn him and his sexy smile that brings visions of pleasurable pain in my future. "Let's get this show on the road, Logan. What are you waiting for? Christmas?" Now I'm getting antsy.

"Jax, I'm going to have him mark you on your left arm. That way we each have one on an opposing arm should we need to close the loop. This will bind us together and keep us safe from any potential traps created by whoever caused the memory removals in the first place."

"Where does that leave me? Let me guess, I'm the middle, right? Wait a second, am I getting two?" When I get Alex back she and I are headed straight to Tribal Tattoo in Hillcrest to ink her up as well. Who am I kidding? She is going to want her own War Eagle original as well. She's sentimental that way.

"Yes. You're the center of this fact-finding mission. We'll be digging into the night Alex left to fight the Demon. After that, we'll jump to a few nights later at your house when all hell broke loose and that friend of hers was killed."

"In self defense, Logan!" Grrr, getting through the story earlier was hard enough without having to listen to his little comments now. "Sounds easy enough." Oh ya, then why am I quaking like an aspen leaf? Knowing that my memory has been altered leaves me feeling violated and completely pissed off. Logan's next question thankfully manages to knock me off that angry course.

"So, um, are you guys roommates?"

"What Logan wants to know, Sandra, is if Alex will be staying there while he's there, right, Logan? You sly dog, you. Leave it to your brother to fall for a girl he's never met. Danger's quite the aphrodisiac for you, right Lo?" Logan tries to brush off the taunts but he can't contain his smile at Jax's nickname for him, or the fact that Jax hit the mark dead on. Boy, I can't wait till this plays out.

"We have to get her back first, lover boy. She may not have long." Logan nods and moves into leader mode.

"Both of you sit in front of the fireplace. Jax, I need you facing me, and Sandra, you can face the fireplace. I'm sure this won't hurt . . . much. I mean, he's willing to help so there won't be the fighting and clawing like before." Oh goody. I'm not afraid of that bird, at least not as much as I am afraid of losing Alex.

"Get on with it, Logan!" Why did I say that? Yi comes at me first. My shoulder blades feel his feathery wind on my back before sizzling hot claws draw patterns over my skin. It's over in an instant, followed by his beak nudging my shoulder in a way that seems like a weird-ass version of a fist bump.

"You good, Sandra?" Jax's eyes are huge watching Yi watching him. The bird's eyes rove over him, marking him like a map. "Easy as pie, big guy. You've had worse." My seductive smile distracts him just in time for Yi to latch on. I am eager to see the result, but I can't take my eyes off of Yi Pollock.

Claws streaking one moment, then pulling back the next, moving from Jax's shoulder to his pec to his back. The bird's graceful maneuvering in such a small space is beyond impressive. Jax's tattoo is more extensive and intricate, that's for sure. More badass, to close the link for what we are going up against—smart move.

The thick tribal black ink shows instantly once Yi breaks away. While the bird returns to Logan, I move to take a better look at Jax. It starts on his shoulder and appears to be a bird's head pointing toward his heart. The eye and beak are the predominant features, subtle, but clear to me. Next, large wings spread across his left pectoral muscle and back over his left shoulder blade. It is intimidating and stunning both in its intricacy and in the process. I'm amazed by the small amount of time and pain the bird had to divvy out to each of us. Jax's would have taken weeks at a parlor and neither of us has any red, swollen areas requiring bandaging and care. While Logan's tattoo looks like the actual eagle, Jax's resembles the totem he has known and treasured most of his life.

I reach behind me and I swear I feel my new wings move under my fingertips, and the look on my face is all it takes for Jax to jump up and head for the mirror. I scramble after him to get a glimpse of the eagle's magic on my skin.

A soft, delicate wing, roughly four inches long, is on each of my shoulder blades. "Oh, Logan. These are beautiful." A birdcall, followed by an annoyed ruffle of feathers, corrects me instantly. "I mean Yi. Thank you."

"Ya, Yi, this is insane. I can feel the bond between us as well, like I know the exact location each of us is on earth. There's no doubt these will keep us safe in the visions." Jax is confident, and the boyish glimmer in his eyes is a sight to behold. My heart twists to think of how long it may have been since he looked like this.

Just like my touch, my wings respond to Jax's touch as well. His fingers tickle along my skin as we both stand mesmerized in front of the mirror. I reach for his totem and the bird stretches his neck and wings. Magic can be quite beautiful sometimes, and this is one of those times. Logan is right. This is going to work.

Back in front of the fireplace, the three of us sit on the floor with our hands on the carpet, our fingers touching. Yi has reclaimed his artistry on Logan's arm, after allowing me to stroke his strong back. I don't fear him any longer, knowing instead that he is going to help us get to Alex.

I close my eyes and focus on moving back through time to the night Alex left for Montana. The jolt into the vision sends chills through me and we are cast back to my house five days ago. Logan, Jax, and I watch the visions of Alex and I talking on the couch, which is exactly what I saw when Dana and I tried this before. Even with those previous attempts, it still rattles me to be me watching, well, me. How did Logan do this over and over again when he tried to find the best way to save me?

I turn to him and watch Yi pull away from his skin and head for the ceiling. Something silver is shimmering above us, which the eagle heads right for. He tears at the threadlike apparition with his claws and beak, making the vision distort in both sight and sound. The thread untangles, unwinds, and then floats slowly toward the floor, changing before our eyes into pieces of wood, flower petals, and leaves that scatter in the air around us before bursting into tiny flames and ash. None of us notices a petal landing lightly on Logan's arm, until its acidic burn sizzles his flesh and makes him let out a curdled scream. Yi flies straight to him and places a foot on the injury. Logan winces at first, but once the eagle lifts off again, all that remains is a puff of smoke and a small area of raised, red skin.

"Okay, so let's move out of the way next time the trippy show starts, deal?" The boys nod my way and we all turn back as the other me looks at something Alex is holding. This is part of what was taken from me, I can tell. I hold my breath as the past me starts to speak.

"Since we still have some time, do you want me to poke around with Justin's stuff?" Yes, I'm starting to remember looking at the items she brought me, and her asking me to look at some of Justin's things. Alex starts to talk and I strain to hear her. *"I'm sure I've been putting him in my dreams lately. I mean, I would've recognized Lestan if he looked like Justin in my dreams long ago, wouldn't I?"* The vision blurs and we return back to the living room with one piece that had been missing.

"Lestan? Wait, I remember her talking about her childhood dreams, and the boy named Lestan who she'd visit in Avalon. She thought they were dreams to help her cope with all the abuse she'd suffered. Her dreams were starting up again, but now Lestan looked like Justin. Shit. I completely remember."

"Lestan the Just Prince? Don't you remember the books we had when we were kids?" Logan starts to pace around gesturing wildly and bordering on a nerdy condescending tone—his "I'm older and know everything" tone that I recognize immediately. "Lestan is the youngest son of the King of Avalon. Does Alex think Justin and Lestan were the same person? Why would a Fae prince be in our world?" My response is to look at Logan like he's the Mad Hatter.

"Okay, smarty-pants. I mustn't have been into what I thought was mostly fictional children's fairytales as much as you were, but I'm guessing you might be right. So, you're saying she's there—Avalon—and that her last words might not have been some dream-fed fear? That maybe Justin was really Lestan the Just Prince?" Why, isn't that clever, that sly asshat.

"Why didn't I get a read on any of Justin's stuff when I checked? I mean nothing! I could have prevented all of this, or at least warned her." Now I'm pacing. Logan stops me and puts his hand on my shoulder, giving it a reassuring squeeze.

"Wild Fae magic is strong, Sandra. If he was the Prince, there must have been plenty of wards in place to keep his identity a secret. Don't waste your energy on worrying about what didn't happen. Save it for what we do moving forward." Back flip, perfect score from my brain-babbling cheerleader. No wonder the FBI wanted him. He is a great leader.

Jax is looking back and forth between us. "Good pep talk! Now, I think we need to be sure of the Avalon thing, guys, so let's look into the day she was taken. There has to be something more that was removed from your memory that can help us." Logan and I agree, and brace for the time I am most afraid of, the one that will reveal an enormous show of dark power.

I focus on the day she disappeared, only two days ago, but it feels so much longer. I remember that I was sitting by her bed, her sleeping form, and what it felt like when she finally woke. Our beach house swims in a blur of color all around us before a stark whiteness takes over. My feet recognize my cool tile floor and I look across the room to see Alex lying in bed, with me by her side. She wakes and the vision blurs and sways, giving me the nauseated feeling and buzzing sound in my ears I got each time Dana and I tried to find out what happened. Yi lifts off again, circling the room, hunting for the thread that has locked up the *truth*. A screech escapes him. We turn to look at the open bedroom door. The entire doorway is like a wicked liquid glass. What monsters are on the other side? It isn't a simple thread this time; whatever this substance is, it is meant to stay put and I wonder if Yi can handle it on his own. My eyes leave the vision knowing that I won't find out anything new unless I destroy the magic that has taken the past from me. I start to walk over to the door with Yi, stopping when Jax grabs my hand.

"Sandra, be careful." I love this man. He's so strong, and he believes in me and in my power; he's got my back. Now let's see if I really can move objects, like Evie, or rather Alana, thinks I can. I don't think it's only a few leaves and shreds of wood this time.

Yi lands on my shoulder and we approach the door together. We hold each other's gaze for a few breaths and then Yi takes off, vicious talons aimed at the heart of the door, and beak wide and dangerous. His attack breaks open the fluid glass and the watery substance transforms into a flock of dark, menacing birds flying right at us among jagged pieces of bark and thorny branches that whip in all directions from the released magic. While Yi dives and tears at the onslaught, I close my eyes and picture the evil vanishing from this place and moving instead into a bleak darkness.

"You are not welcome here. This is *my* memory, from *my* mind. This is my life. Now, begone!" When my eyes open, the crazed tornado of wild magic binds together and rises to the ceiling before freezing in place. I look at my raptor companion and in the next second the mass dives toward us. My voice rings out while the war eagle shrieks along with me.

"I said *leave this place!*" Hands slip into mine. Jax and Logan join me in a show of force and power. I see the tattoos on their bodies ignite like silver fire, just as I feel warmth gathering where mine are. I will not flinch. This will work—it has to. Five feet, four, three, two . . . a crack like breaking lightning is followed by silence and emptiness above us.

"Hell ya, Sandra." But I have already released Jax and Logan's hands, instead crossing the room in a full-out sprint toward the vision scene that is playing out between Alex and the past me. Alex is talking to the past me when I see myself suddenly stiffen in the bedside chair. Now I am left to watch in horror as I launch myself at her. What the hell was I doing? But then my own words echo in my head as vision me whispers them to her, as I remember.

> *Fairy fingertips tickle my toes.*
> *Lights of the pale moonlight haunt my dreams.*
> *Where has the boy gone, the boy who is more than he*
>   *seems?*
> *Only the King knows and he is after me.*

Chills run up my spine as I recall the invasion in my head and the dangerous words dripping from my lips. The next few seconds are torturous when an immense gust of wild energy rushes through me before the room goes black and Alex is gone. Guilt and grief overwhelms me, but I manage to gather myself enough to prepare our return to the beach house. As I feel the first trickles of the vision fading, Yi comes to me and holds tight to my shoulders, one clawed foot on each tattooed wing. I instantly hear Alex's thoughts, not a current stream of consciousness, but what she was thinking as she was taken away, freezing me in my anguish.

"I'm alone. Payment for the sin is due and now Lestan's father is coming for me. AVALON! He's taking me to Avalon. Please find me."

The eagle's weight lifts off me and I kneel to the ground. The amount of power I have used and the sheer gravity of what was taken from my memory, of possibly having been used for more than just the bearer of words, and of the understanding that now I know for sure where she is, hits me. But something else strikes a blow, too. We have defeated this Fae magic, this lingering influence from the Fae king of Avalon—and we are all going back to Cali to find her and bring her home together. Logan, Yi, Jax, Dana . . . all of us, and we *are* bringing her back.

The vision fades and we are back in Sandbridge. When I rise and look at the boys, I can't contain my smile. Jax speaks first, his eyes shining with excitement. "So let me see if I can spin this crazy tale right. Your girl is in fairyland and we think her ex-boyfriend's dad is the king who took her there to punish her for his son's death? Sounds like a blast, if a tad bit crazy. Guess I better call the office." When Jax walks away I turn and hug Logan.

"I always believed you had some major skill, Sandra, but that was incredible. And you and Yi working together? There are going to be dangers ahead, ones that I'm sure will be more brutal than this, but now we have a taste of what we can do. I'm also pretty sure the king felt his wards fall today, so I hope he's scared." Oh. I hadn't thought about that.

"That means he may know we're coming. Shit, what if he moves her or hurts her?"

"He obviously wants something from her. He blames Alex for Justin's, or rather Lestan's, death. We need to get with your other friends and find a way to her, that is, if we can't just get there ourselves." I love confidant Logan. He isn't obsessing with power or his Sight; he's just eager to help. For the first time in a long time we're going to do some real good together. At least it wasn't Demons again. I had been so crossing my fingers and toes that a Demon didn't have her.

"Nope, not a Demon, folks. I kicked that sucker's ass till his last molecule." Logan jumps a bit and I know he heard her, too. Linking together with Yi may have linked us all to Alex. Cool. *"So, my memory is back. I know where I am. Justin's, uh, Lestan's dad has me. Freaking crazy-ass king doesn't know how to host very well. He blames me for Justin's death, but there's something he wants. I don't know what it is for sure, yet."*

Yep, I am almost positive she killed our Demon. We are all free from the burden of revenge and this foul-mouthed vixen is to thank. I swallow hard, still worried by the vision of my body and mind being used by the king. What if he used my gifts as well? What if I am the reason he was able to move her to Avalon? Only one good thing comes out of this fear. If I moved her once, I can move her again.

"Alex, this is Logan. Can you hold this connection for as long as possible? I want to see if it lets Sandra and I enter a vision of you in Avalon. I'm not sure if we can get there in the present, so it may be the past or future, but whatever the case, it can help us find your exact location."

"Okay, big boy, anything for you." Logan grabs my hand and I shout for Jax who heads back into the room.

"Since we're heading out of this world, I think it's best that you stay grounded for us here, Jax. Just in case you need to bring us back. The Nanda-yi marks will keep us tethered, so don't worry. You can call us back." Jax nods and gives my hand a squeeze and my cheek a sweet kiss.

"Focus on Alex, Sandra. Alex, keep talking to us." Her voice carries into my mind while Yi hovers in front of us, facing us with white eyes. His wings fan me, calming the heat that has become unbearable under my anxiety. I feel the world drop away around us, but still feel my connection to Jax pulsing from my right wing. A cold, damp darkness becomes our backdrop. I see flickering candlelight off to the right and a muffling of voices rises over the stillness. Logan and I walk toward the soft noise when suddenly a booming voice breaks through the calm of the vision.

"*Either call her to you, Eila, or I will send you to her shackled and make you bring her back, and trust me, you won't like how that option feels or what I will do once you both return.*" Logan and I rush toward the voice, Yi flying above us. A dark, cold, metal cell comes into view and a tall, forbidding figure stands outside the bars. He is dressed in a long, dark-green cape, and although the darkness hides many things, there is no denying the marks of royalty in the glittering gemstones and golden threads woven throughout the garment. I look him over some more and notice a crown formed from interwoven metal tree branches resting on his head. It too is covered in dazzling gems.

"That must be the king," I whisper to Logan, although I know we can't be heard. I wonder if this is a vision of the future, something that has already come to pass, or whether it might be the present. I am hoping for the latter, because I may have a plan.

A smaller person stands tall and defiant in the cage, but then slumps suddenly and turns away. The king paces along the outside of the cell, his hands clasped casually behind him, while inside, wearing tattered clothes and standing on a bare stone floor, is Alex. The king moves closer to the bars and hisses, dropping his relaxed demeanor to reveal his sinister nature.

"You will wither away in here, Eila. No, you won't die, at least not quickly, but I can make you suffer away your days—that you can be certain of. And when I find her and you are no more, I'll bring her down here to sift through your dust and brittle, broken bones!" Quicker than I can utter a curse, Alex lunges at the king, her long arm shooting out through the bars and scratching at his face. She may be suffering in there, but she is still fighting and she may have even struck him. The king laughs as Alex screams in pain. A red circle forms on her wrist and I step closer to see a bracelet alight like a hot coal. When Alex yanks her arm back into the cell, the fiery, cursed trinket loses its flame.

"Well, well now. Aren't we still a feisty mortal. Maybe you'll have no meals today; that should teach you a lesson. You still think help is coming, don't you? Never, Eila, no one will ever find you. I have made certain of it." Logan takes my hand and squeezes it.

"We'll get her out of here, Sandra. Let's take a look around and see if we can find anything else that can tell us exactly where she is."

"Why don't I try to take her now? You said yourself that I can move objects through dimensions. Maybe I can move a person as well. Maybe I already have." Logan shoots a confused look my way, but then realization hits him. The only trick is to be certain that this is a vision of the present. I try to speak to Alex, but she isn't responding.

"Or maybe the two of you can stay here with her." The words freeze us, except for our heads that swivel toward the king. He is looking right at us and there is no doubt in my mind that he sees us as plain as day. We are in a present vision, we have to be. Yi lets out a screech and places his body between us. The king steps in our direction and with a flick of his hand sends the gigantic eagle backward.

"What do you say, Oman twins? You will make excellent additions to my collection." I can't move and the king continues to inch closer, pointing at us with a wicked-looking finger. An orbed ring sits behind his knuckle, glowing a deep red and pulsing in the darkness. Oh my god we have to get out of here, but Alex. I have to get Alex.

"Sandra, get out of here. Please, Sandra. Leave now before he takes you, too." Alex's eyes lock on mine and the pleading and determination within them etch into my brain. I speak to her with still lips while Yi moves next to me.

"We'll be back, Alex, I promise. Jax, bring us home, quick." I squeeze Logan's hand and Yi launches past the king to Alex. He does an acrobatic fly-by along the bars of Alex's prison, returns to us in a blink of an eye, and we are gone. Her words drift after me in the blurring of time and space.

"Come back for me."

CHAPTER 11

In the Air

It feels good to be heading back west. We are going to meet with the entire San Diego crew to hash out a plan to get Alex back. Yi had given her one of his feathers during his spectacular maneuver and Logan has been practicing honing in on her location and using that link to hear what is going on, wherever she may be. That way we can make sure we are alone next time. Dana had been more than a little livid about what we had nearly succumbed to in the vision.

"Damn children need to learn to take precautions and seek guidance before jumping in naked and all hopped up on sex and newfound fuzzy forgiveness feelings." Yep, I sure have missed her.

This flight is already one hundred times better than the one I took when I left after college. Especially since I know that Jax is coming out tomorrow, and I have Logan in the seat next to me, ready to help me save Alex. We have been talking about the Demon Alex took down and how Logan can't wait to talk to her in person about what she did. When he isn't testing the new connection Yi's feather affords us, he wanders into the vision of her destroying the hideous creature that nearly destroyed her father. Well, nearly destroyed all of us. Logan can tell without a doubt that it was our Demon.

"I thought I wanted that victory alone—I have been driven by revenge for all these years. Yes, the training at the FBI helped me to keep from letting the rage take over, but I'm glad that Demon met his match with Alex. Who knows what kind of person I would've become if I allowed all that fury and vengeance loose." Having Alex be the one to do the deed thrills Logan. He has never properly met her, but I can tell already that he is falling for her—and hard.

Still, nothing like your twin sister's deception to ruin the moment for you; two bombshells are about to be dropped that will turn this into one memorable flight. A third can stay put for a while; I am not even sure what's going on between her and Ryan so no need to squash Logan's hopes just yet.

"Er, Logan, I have a couple of things to tell you. I think it's best to do it now that we're roughly thirty thousand feet above ground and, uh, in a very public situation. You have to promise to keep an open mind, and whatever you do, do not freak out." He rolls his eyes at me and crosses his arms.

"Come on, Sandra. I'm not like that. The FBI trained me to handle any situation, so lay it on me." Well, okay, he asked for it.

"So you know Alana, Evie, or whatever her name is? Well, I'm ninety-nine point nine percent sure that she's Alex's mom, Stacy Conner." His eyes widen but he doesn't seem particularly fazed. "And two?" He takes a look at the non-watch on his arm to show he isn't rattled. Oh man, he is going to flip out.

"And two, you know Valant, the guy I told you killed Justin, or Lestan I guess we should call him now. Anyhow, remember how Valant did it to protect Alex?"

"Yes, Sandra. What about him?"

"Well—he's a Demon."

"He's a *what? Sandra!*"

Yep, this is going to be a long flight.

Thank you for reading
Forbidden: An Alex Conner Chronicles Novella

Be sure to pick up the first two books of the Alex Conner Chronicles series:
Trust: The Alex Conner Chronicles Book One
&
Truth: The Alex Conner Chronicles Book Two

Only: The Alex Conner Chronicles Books Three, is coming soon so follow me on my social media platforms to stay up to date! And don't forget to check out my website and follow me on

Facebook, Instagram, Talnts & Twitter.

www.ParkerSinclair.net
Facebook: ParkerSinclairbooks
Instagram: @ParkerSinclairAuthor
Twitter: Parker_Sinclair
Talnts: @ParkerSinclair

I would like to thank the following research sites for the excellent information that helped shape the Nanda-yi's (Yi's) character.

Wildspeak:
www.wildspeak.com/animalenergies/eaglewedgetailed.html

The Wagman Online Dictionary:
sydney.edu.au/arts/linguistics/research/wagiman/dict/dict.html

About the Author

Ms. Sinclair gives credit to the development of her imagination and passion for writing to multiple childhood destinations lacking indoor plumbing. It may sound odd, yet when your journey to adulthood consists of numerous backpacking, camping, and hiking  trips to the most out-of-the-way and breathtakingly beautiful places in North America, the creation of games, worlds, and characters are the results. She would never trade the childhood her parents gave her, and she thanks them for raising her to have her own thoughts, dreams, and bountiful imagination. Oh and she wishes to thank them for teaching her that one should never leave their jeans on the floor of an everglades campground shower—lest they do the dance of the scorpions in the pants again!

While attending college, Ms. Sinclair studied biological sciences and psychology, specifically animal behavior, but her love has forever been to write. There are boxes in her house filled with notebooks, journals, and logs with poems, stories, lyrics, and personal rants scratched into them with pencil, marker, pen, whatever she could get her hands on. Words demanded to be thrown out of her mind and onto paper by any means necessary. Ms. Sinclair's studies have contributed greatly to the worlds, characters, and stories she creates, proving that no matter what path you take, it will all be part of where you end up—sometimes in spectacular ways!

Since 2007, Ms. Sinclair calls Virginia Beach home where she is employed as a full-time educational counselor, and finding time to write late into the night after her kiddos, and in many cases, her husband, are fast asleep.

Made in the USA
Middletown, DE
25 January 2017